All's Well

Emily Sarah Holt

DODO
PRESS

All's Well

Chapter One.

Friends and neighbours.

"Give you good-morrow, neighbour! Whither away with that great fardel (Bundle), prithee?"

"Truly, Mistress, home to Staplehurst, and the fardel holdeth broadcloth for my lads' new jerkins." The speakers were two women, both on the younger side of middle age, who met on the road between Staplehurst and Cranbrook, the former coming towards Cranbrook and the latter from it. They were in the midst of that rich and beautiful tract of country known as the Weald of Kent, once the eastern part of the great Andredes Weald, a vast forest which in Saxon days stretched from Kent to the border of Hampshire. There was still, in 1556, much of the forest about the Weald, and even yet it is a well-wooded part of the country, the oak being its principal tree, though the beech sometimes grows to an enormous size. Trees of the Weald were sent to Rome for the building of Saint Peter's.

"And how go matters with you, neighbour?" asked the first speaker, whose name was Alice Benden.

"Well, none so ill," was the reply. "My master's in full work, and we've three of our lads at the cloth-works. We're none so bad off as some."

"I marvel how it shall go with Sens Bradbridge, poor soul! She'll be bad off enough, or I err greatly."

"Why, how so, trow? I've not heard what ails her."

"Dear heart! then you know not poor Benedict is departed?"

"Eh, you never mean it!" exclaimed the bundle-bearer, evidently shocked. "Why, I reckoned he'd taken a fine turn toward recovery. Well, be sure! Ay, poor Sens, I'm sorry for her."

"Two little maids, neither old enough to earn a penny, and she a stranger in the town, pretty nigh, with never a 'quaintance saving them near about her, and I guess very few pennies in her purse. Ay, 'tis a sad look-out for Sens, poor heart."

"Trust me, I'll look in on her, and see what I may do, so soon as I've borne this fardel home. Good lack! but the burying charges 'll come heavy on her! and I doubt she's saved nought, as you say, Benedict being sick so long."

"I scarce think there's much can be done," said Alice, as she moved forward; "I was in there of early morrow, and Barbara Final, she took the maids home with her. But a kindly word's not like to come amiss. Here's Emmet (See Note 1) Wilson at hand: she'll bear you company home, for I have ado in the town. Good-morrow, Collet."

"Well, good-morrow, Mistress Benden. I'll rest my fardel a bit on the stile while Emmet comes up."

And, lifting her heavy bundle on the stile, Collet Pardue wiped her heated face with one end of her mantle—there were no shawls in those days—and waited for Emmet Wilson to come up.

Emmet was an older woman than either Alice or Collet, being nearly fifty years of age. She too carried a bundle, though not of so formidable a size. Both had been to Cranbrook, then the centre of the cloth-working industry, and its home long before the days of machinery. There were woven the solid grey broadcloths which gave to the men of the Weald the title of "the Grey-Coats of Kent." From all the villages round about, the factory-hands were recruited. The old factories had stood from the days when Edward the Third and his Flemish Queen brought over the weavers of the Netherlands to improve the English manufactures; and some of them stand yet, turned into ancient residences for the country squires who had large stakes in them in the old days, or peeping out here and there in the principal streets of the town, in the form of old gables and other antique adornments.

"Well, Collet! You've a brave fardel yonder!"

"I've six lads and two lasses, neighbour," said Collet with a laugh. "Takes a sight o' cloth, it do, to clothe 'em."

"Be sure it do! Ay, you've a parcel of 'em. There's only my man and Titus at our house. Wasn't that Mistress Benden that parted from you but now? She turned off a bit afore I reached her."

"Ay, it was. She's a pleasant neighbour."

"She's better than pleasant, she's good."

"Well, I believe you speak sooth. I'd lief you could say the same of her master. I wouldn't live with Master Benden for a power o' money."

"Well, I'd as soon wish it too, for Mistress Benden's body; but I'm not so certain sure touching Mistress Benden's soul. 'Tis my belief if Master Benden were less cantankerous, Mistress wouldn't be nigh so good."

"What, you hold by the old rhyme, do you—?

"'A spaniel, a wife, and a walnut tree,

The more they be beaten, the better they be.'"

"Nay, I'll not say that: but this will I say, some folks be like camomile—'the more you tread it, the more you spread it.' When you squeeze 'em, like clover, you press the honey forth: and I count Mistress Benden's o' that sort."

"Well, then, let's hope poor Sens Bradbridge is likewise, for she's like to get well squeezed and trodden. Have you heard she's lost her master?"

"I have so. Mistress Final told me this morrow early. Nay, I doubt she's more of the reed family, and 'll bow down her head like a bulrush. Sens Bradbridge'll bend afore she breaks, and Mistress Benden 'll break afore she bends."

"'Tis pity Mistress Benden hath ne'er a child; it might soften her master, and anyhow should comfort her."

"I wouldn't be the child," said Emmet drily.

Collet laughed. "Well, nor I neither," said she. "I reckon they'll not often go short of vinegar in that house; Master Benden's face 'd turn all the wine, let alone the cream. I'm fain my master's not o' that fashion: he's a bit too easy, my Nick is. I can't prevail on him to thwack the lads when they're over-thwart; I have to do it myself."

"I'll go bail you'd not hurt 'em much," said Emmet, with an amused glance at the round, rosy, good-humoured face of the mother of the six "over-thwart" lads.

"Oh, will you! But I am a short mistress with 'em, I can tell you. Our Aphabell shall hear of it, I promise you, when I get home. I bade him yester-even fetch me two pound o' prunes from the spicer's, and gave him threepence in his hand to pay for 'em; and if the rascal went not and lost the money at cross and pile with Gregory White, and never a prune have I in the store-cupboard. He's at all evers playing me tricks o' that fashion. 'Tisn't a week since I sent him for a dozen o' Paris candles, and he left 'em in the water as he came o'er the bridge. Eh, Mistress Wilson, but lads be that pestiferous! You've but one, and that one o' the quiet peaceable sort—you've somewhat to be thankful for, I can tell you, that hasn't six like me, and they a set o' contrarious, outrageous, boisterous caitiffs as ever was seen i' this world."

"Which of 'em would you wish to part with, Collet?"

"Well, be sure!" was Collet's half-laughing answer, as she mentally reviewed the young gentlemen in question—her giddy, thoughtless Aphabell, her mischievous Tobias, her Esdras always out at elbows, her noisy, troublesome Noah, her rough Silvanus, whom no amount of "thwacking" seemed to polish, and her lazy, ease-loving Valentine. "Nay, come, I reckon I'll not make merchandise of any of 'em this bout. They are a lot o' runagates, I own, but I'm their mother, look you."

Emmet Wilson smiled significantly. "Ay, Collet, and 'tis well for you and me that cord bears pulling at."

"You and me?" responded Collet, lifting her bundle higher, into an easier position. "'Tis well enough for the lads, I dare say; but what ado hath it with you and me?"

"I love to think, neighbour, that somewhat akin to it is said by nows and thens of us, too, in the Court of the Great King, when the enemy accuseth us—'Ay, she did this ill thing, and she's but a poor black sinner at best; but thou shalt not have her, Satan; I'm her Father.'"

"You're right there, Emmet Wilson," said Collet, in a tone which showed that the last sentence had touched her heart. "The work and care that my lads give me is nought to the sins wherewith we be daily angering the Lord. He's always forgiving us, be sure."

"A sight easier than men do, Collet Pardue, take my word for it."

"What mean you, neighbour?" asked Collet, turning round to look her companion in the face, for Emmet's tone had indicated that she meant more than she said.

"I mean one man in especial, and his name's Bastian."

"What, the priest? Dear heart! I've not angered him, trow?"

"You soon will, *if* you cut your cloth as you've measured it. How many times were you at mass this three months past?"

"How many were you?" was the half-amused answer.

"There's a many in Staplehurst as hasn't been no oftener," said Emmet, "that I know: but it'll not save you, Collet. The priest has his eye on you, be sure."

"Then I'll keep mine on him," said Collet sturdily, as she paused at her own door, which was that of the one little shoemaker's shop in the village of Staplehurst. "Good-morrow, neighbour. I'll but lay down my fardel, and then step o'er to poor Sens Bradbridge."

"And I'll come to see her this even. Good-morrow."

And Emmet Wilson walked on further to her home, where her husband was the village baker and corn-monger.

Note 1. Emmet is a very old variation of Emma, and sometimes spelt Emmot; Sens is a corruption of Sancha, naturalised among us in the thirteenth century; and Collet or Colette, the diminutive of Nichola, a common and favourite name in the Middle Ages.

Chapter Two.

Christabel.

Alice Benden had reached Cranbrook, and was busied with her various errands. Her position was slightly superior to that of Emmet and Collet, for she was the wife of a man who "lived upright," which enigmatical expression signified that he had not to work for his living. Edward Benden's father had made a little money, and his son, who had no children to whom to leave his property, chose to spend it rather than bequeath it to distant relatives who were strangers to him. He owned some half-dozen houses at Staplehurst, one of which was occupied by the Pardues, and he lived on the rents of these, and the money saved by his thrifty father. The rents he asked were not unreasonable, but if a tenant failed to pay, out he must go. He might as well appeal to the door-posts as to Edward Benden.

This agreeable gentleman treated his wife much as he did his tenants. He gave a sum of money into her hands for certain purchases, and with that sum those purchases must be made. It was not of the least use to explain failure by an unexpected rise in prices, or the fact that the article required could not be had at a given time. Mr Benden expected perfection—in every one but himself. Excuses, many and often very poor, were admitted for that favoured individual, but no other had a chance to offer any.

On the present occasion, Alice had ten shillings for her marketing, with which she was expected to provide six rabbits, a dozen pigeons, twenty-four eggs, five yards of buckram, a black satin cap and a brown silk doublet for her husband, a pair of shoes for herself, and sundry things at the spicer's. The grocer, or grosser, as the word was originally spelt, only sold wholesale, and his stock as we have it was divided among the spicer, pepperer, and treacle-monger. That her money would not stretch thus far Alice well knew, and she knew also that if she were to avoid a scolding, Mr Benden's personal wants must be supplied, whatever became of her own. Her first call, therefore, was at the capper's for the satin cap, which cost one shilling and eightpence; then at the tailor's for the doublet, which took four and sixpence; then she paid ninepence for the pigeons, which were for Mr Benden's personal eating; and next she went to the spicer's. A sugarloaf she must have, expensive as it was, for her tyrant required his dishes sweet, and demanded that the result should be effected by dainty sugar, not like common people by honey or treacle: nor did she dare to omit the currants, since he liked currant cake with his cheese and ale. Two pounds of prunes, and four of rice, she meant to add; but those were not especially for him, and must be left out if needful. When she had reached this point, Alice paused, and counted up what money she had left.

"Doublet, 4 shillings 6 pence; cap, 1 shilling 8 pence; pigeons, 9 pence; sugarloaf, 7 pence; currants, 1 shilling: total, 8 shillings 6 pence." Thus ran Alice's calculations. "Only eighteenpence left. The other things I wanted will come to 6 shillings 9 pence. What can I do without?"

The buckram must go: that was the heaviest article in the list, five yards at ninepence a yard. Alice's Sunday gown must be worn without a new lining for a while longer. Two rabbits instead of six, at twopence a piece; three pennyworth of eggs at eight a penny: these she could scarcely do without. The shoes, too, were badly wanted. Rice and prunes could not be had to-day. Alice bought a pair of cheaper shoes than she intended, paying tenpence instead of a shilling; purchased the two rabbits and the eggs; and found that she had one penny left. She decided that this would answer her purpose—nay, it must do so. Mr Benden was not likely to ask if she had all she needed, so long as she did not fail to supply his own requirements. She arranged with the poulterer to put by the rabbits, pigeons, and eggs, for which she would send a boy in the afternoon; and carrying the rest of her parcels, with which she was well laden, she took the road to Staplehurst.

As she turned the corner of the last house in Cranbrook, she was brought to a stand-still by a voice behind her.

"Alice!"

A light sprang to Alice's eyes as she turned quickly round to greet a man a few years older than herself—a man with grave dark eyes and a brown beard. Passing all her parcels into the left hand, she gave him the right—an action which at that time was an indication of intimate friendship. The kiss and the hand-clasp have changed places since then.

"Why, Roger! I look not to see thee now. How goes it this morrow with Christie?"

"As the Lord will, good sister."

"And that, mefeareth, is but evil?"

"Nay, I will not lay that name on aught the Lord doth. But she suffers sorely, poor darling! Wilt come round our way and look in on her, Alice?"

"I would I might, Roger!" said Alice, with a rather distressed look. "But this morrow—"

"Thou hast not good conveniency thereto." Roger finished the sentence for her. "Then let be till thine occasion serveth. Only, when it so doth, bethink thee that a look on Aunt Alice is a rare comfort to the little maid."

"Be thou sure I shall not forget it. Tom came in last night, Roger. He and Tabitha and the childre, said he, fare well."

"That's a good hearing. And Edward hath his health?"

"Oh ay, Edward doth rarely well."

Mr Benden was not apt to lose his health, which partly accounted for the very slight sympathy he was wont to show with those who were. It was noticeable that while other people were spoken of by affectionate diminutives both from Alice and her brother, Edward and Tabitha received their names in full.

"Well, then, Alice, I shall look for thee—when thou shalt be able to come. The Lord have thee in His keeping!"

"The Lord be with thee, dear Roger!"

And Roger Hall turned down a side street, while Alice went on toward Staplehurst. They were deeply attached to each other, this brother and sister, and all the more as they found little sympathy outside their mutual affection. Roger was quite aware of Alice's home troubles, and she of his. They could see but little of each other, for while Mr Benden had not absolutely forbidden his brother-in-law to enter his house, it was a familiar fact to all parties that his sufficiently sharp temper was not softened by a visit from Roger Hall, and Alice's sufferings from the temper in question were generally enough to prevent her from trying it further. It was not only sharp, but also uncertain. What pleased him to-day—and few things did please him—was by no means sure to please him to-morrow. Alice trod on a perpetual volcano, which was given to opening and engulfing her just at the moment when she least expected it.

Roger's home troubles were of another sort. His wife was dead, and his one darling was his little Christabel, whose few years had hitherto been passed in pain and suffering. The apothecary was not able to find out what hidden disorder sapped the spring of little Christie's health, and made her from her very babyhood a frail, weak, pallid invalid, scarcely fit to do anything except lie on a sofa, learn a few little lessons from her father, and amuse herself with fancy work. A playfellow she could seldom bear. Her cousins, the three daughters of her Uncle Thomas, who lived about a mile away, were too rough and noisy for the frail child, with one exception—Justine, who was lame, and could not keep up with the rest. But Justine was not a comfortable companion, for she possessed a grumbling temper, or it would perhaps be more correct to say she was possessed by it. She suffered far less than Christie, yet Christie was always bright and sunny, while Justine was dark and cloudy. Yet not even Justine tried Christie as did her Aunt Tabitha.

Aunt Tabitha was one of those women who wish and mean to do a great deal of good, and cannot tell how to do it. Not that she realised that inability by any means. She was absolutely convinced that nearly all the good done in the Weald of Kent was done by Tabitha Hall, while the real truth was that if Tabitha Hall had been suddenly transported to Botany Bay, or any other distant region, the Weald of Kent would have got along quite as well without her. According to Aunt Tabitha, the one grand duty of every human creature was to rouse himself and other people: and, measured by this rule, Aunt Tabitha certainly did her duty. She earnestly impressed on Alice that Mr Benden would develop into a perfect angel if only she stood up to him; and she was never tired of assuring Christie that her weakness and suffering were entirely the result of her own idle disinclination to rouse herself. Thus urged, Christie did sometimes try to rouse herself, the result being that when deprived of the stimulating presence of Aunt Tabitha, she was fit for nothing but bed for some time afterwards. It was a good thing for her that Aunt Tabitha's family kept her busy at home for the most part, so that her persecutions of poor Christie were less frequent than they would otherwise have been.

Mr Thomas Hall, the younger brother of Roger and Alice, had the air of a man who had been stood up to, until he had lost all power or desire of standing up for himself. He remarked that it was a fine morning with an aspect of deprecation that would have made it seem quite cruel to disagree with him, even if it were raining hard. He never contradicted his Tabitha: poor man, he knew too well what would come of it! It would have been as easy for him to walk up to the mouth of a loaded cannon when the gunner was applying the match, as to remark to her, in however mild a tone, that he preferred his mutton boiled when he knew she liked it roasted. Yet he was a good man, in his meek unobtrusive way, and Christie liked her Uncle Thomas next best to her father and Aunt Alice.

"Christie, I marvel you are not weary!" said her lively, robust cousin Friswith (a corruption of Frideawide), one day.

Not weary! Ah, how little Friswith knew about it!

"I am by times, Friswith," said Christie meekly.

"Mother saith she is assured you might have better health an' you would. You lie and lie there like a log of wood. Why get you not up and go about like other folks?"

"I can't, cousin; it hurts me."

"Hurts you, marry! I wouldn't give in to a bit of a hurt like that! I never mind being hurt."

Christie silently doubted that last statement.

"Hear you, Christie?"

"Yes, Friswith, I hear."

"Then why rouse you not up, as Mother saith?"

"I can't, Friswith; my head pains me this morrow."

"Lack-a-daisy, what a fuss you make o'er a bit of pain! Well, I must be away—I've to go to Cranbrook of an errand for Mother; she lacks a sarcenet coif. If I can scrimp enough money out of this, I'll have some carnation ribbon to guard my hat—see if I don't!"

"Oh, Friswith! It isn't your money, 'tis Aunt Tabitha's."

"I'll have it, though; I hate to go shabby. And I can tell you, I met Beatrice Pardue last night, with a fresh ribbon on hers. I'll not have her finer than me. She's stuck-up enough without it. You look out on Sunday as I go by the window, and see if my hat isn't new guarded with carnation. I'll get round Mother somehow; and if she do give me a whipping, I'm not so soft as you. Good-morrow!"

"Friswith, don't!"

Friswith only laughed as she closed the door on Christabel, and ran off lightly down the Cranbrook road.

Chapter Three.

The comfortable Justice.

Mr Justice Roberts sat in his dining-room after supper, with a tankard of ale at his elbow. Had the "pernicious weed" been discovered at that date, he would probably also have had a pipe in his hand; but tobacco being yet a calamity of the future, the Justice was not smoking.

He was, however, very comfortable. He sat in a big leather chair, which rested his portly figure; he had just had a good supper, consisting of a partridge pie and a dish of juicy pears; he had sold a horse that morning at considerable profit; his mind was as easy as his body.

There was only one thing the occurrence of which Mr Roberts would have thought it worth his while to deprecate at that moment. This was, anybody coming to bother him. The worthy Justice did not like to be bothered. A good many people are of the same opinion. He had that evening but one enemy in the world, and that was the man who should next rap at his house door.

"Rap-a-tap-tap-tap!"

"Go to Jericho!" said the Justice to the unseen individual who was thus about to disturb his rest. "I want none of you. Why on earth can't you let a man alone?—What is it, Martha?"

"Please you, Master, 'tis Master Benden would have a word with you."

"What can the companion want?" mildly growled the Justice. "Well! let him in, and bring another tankard. Good evening, Master Benden. A fine autumn eve, trow."

Mr Benden's face said that he had come to talk about something of more moment than autumn evenings. He sat down opposite the Justice, buttoned his long gown up to the neck, as if to gird himself for action, and cleared his throat with an air of importance.

"Master Roberts, I am come on a grave matter and a sad."

"Can't deal with grave matters after supper," said the Justice. "Come again in the morning. Take a pear."

"Sir, this is a serious business."

"Business hours are over. I never do business out of hours."

"To-night, Master Roberts, and to-night only, shall serve for this business."

"I do no business out of hours!" solemnly repeated the officer of the law. "Take a pear—take two pears, and come again in the morning."

Mr Benden shook his head in a tragic manner, and let the pears alone.

"They are good pears," said the Justice. "If you love no pears, put one in your pocket with my commendations to good Mistress Benden. How doth she?—well, I hope."

"Were I able, Sir," replied the visitor impressively, "to bear your commendations to good Mistress Benden, I were the happier man. But, alas! I am not at that pass."

"What, come you hither to complain of your wife? Fie, Master Benden! Go you home and peace her, like a wise man as you are, and cast her half a suffering for some woman's gear."

Mr Benden might most truthfully have made reply that he had ere that evening bestowed on his wife not half a suffering only, but many whole ones: but he knew that the Justice meant half a sovereign, which was then pronounced exactly like suffering.

"Sir!" he said rather angrily, "it pleases you to reckon lightly of this matter: but what, I pray you, if you have to make account thereon with the Queen's Grace's laws, not to speak of holy Church? Sir, I give you to wit that my wife is an ill hussy, and an heretic belike, and lacketh a sharp pulling up—sharper than I can give her. She will not go to church, neither hear mass, nor hath she shriven her this many a day. You are set in office, methinks, to administer the laws, and have no right thus to shuffle off your duty by hours and minutes. I summon you to perform it in this case."

Mr Justice Roberts was grave enough now. The half-lazy, half-jocose tone which he had hitherto worn was cast aside entirely, and the expression of his face grew almost stern. But the sternness was not all for the culprit thus arraigned before him; much of it was for the prosecutor. He was both shocked and disgusted with the course Mr Benden had taken: which course is not fiction, but fact.

"Master Benden," said he, "I am two men—the Queen's officer of her laws, and plain Anthony Roberts of Cranbrook. You speak this even but to Anthony Roberts: and as such, good Master, I would have you bethink you that if your wife be brought afore me as Justice, I must deal with her according to law. You know, moreover, that in case she shall admit her guilt, and refuse to amend, there is no course open to me save to commit her to prison: and you know, I suppose, what the end of that may be. Consider well if you are avised to go through with it. A man need count the cost of building an house ere he layeth in a load of bricks."

"You are not wont, Master Justice, to be thus tender over women," said Benden derisively. "Methinks ere now I have heard you to thank the saints you never wedded one."

"And may do so yet again, Master Benden. I covet little to have a wife to look after."

Like many men in his day, Mr Roberts looked upon a wife not as somebody who would look after him, in the sense of making him comfortable, but rather as one whom he would have the trouble of perpetually keeping out of all sorts of ways that were naughty and wrong.

"But that is not your case," he continued in the same stern tone. "You set to-night—if you resolve to persevere therein—a ball rolling that may not tarry till it reach the fire. Are you avised thereon?"

"I am. Do your duty!" was the savage reply.

"Then do you yours," said Mr Roberts coldly, "and bring Mrs Benden before me next sessions day. There is time to forethink you ere it come."

Unconscious of the storm thus lowering over her, Alice Benden was sitting by little Christie's sofa. There were then few playthings, and no children's books, and other books were scarce and costly. Fifty volumes was considered a large library, and in few houses even of educated people were there more books than about half-a-dozen. For an invalid confined to bed or sofa, whether child or adult, there was little resource save needlework. Alice had come to bring her little niece a roll of canvas and some bright-coloured silks. Having so much time to spare, and so little variety of occupation, Christie was a more skilful embroideress than many older women. A new pattern was a great pleasure, and there were few pleasures open to the invalid and lonely child. Her sole home company was her father, for their one servant, Nell, was too busy, with the whole work of the house upon her hands, to do more for Christabel than necessity required; and Mr Hall, who was manager of one of the large factories in Cranbrook, was obliged to be away nearly the whole day. Other company—her Aunt Alice excepted—was rather a trial than a pleasure to Christabel. The young people were rough and noisy, even when they tried not to be so, and the child's nerves were weak. Aunt Tabitha worried her to "rouse herself, and not be a burden on her poor father"; and how gladly would Christabel have done it! Uncle Thomas was also a harassing visitor, though in another way.

He never knew what to say, when he had once asked how the invalid felt: he only sat and gazed at her and the window alternately, now and then, as though by a mental jerk, bringing out a few words.

"He causes me to feel so naughty, Aunt," said Christie dolefully, "and I do want to be good. He sits and looks on me till I feel—I feel—Aunt Alice, I can't find the words: as if all my brains would come out of my finger-ends, if he went on. And now and then he says a word or two—such as 'Rain afore night, likely,' or 'Bought a drove of pigs yesterday,' and I can only say, 'Yes, uncle.' I think 'tis hard for both of us, Aunt Alice, for we don't know what to say one to the other. I can't talk to *him*, and he can't talk to *me*."

Alice laughed, and then the tears almost rose in her eyes, as she softly smoothed Christie's fair hair. She knew full well the sensation of intense, miserable nerve-strain, for which the little girl strove in vain to find words.

"'Tis hard to be patient, little Christie," she said tenderly. "But God knoweth it, dear heart; and He is very patient with us."

"O Aunt Alice, I know! And I am so sorry afterwards, when I should have been quiet and patient, and I have spoken crossly. People know not how hard it is, and how hard one tries: they only see when one gives way. They see not even how ashamed one is afterwards."

"Truth, sweet heart; but the Lord seeth."

"Aunt, think you the Lord Jesus ever felt thus?"

"He never felt sin, Christie; but I reckon He knew as well as any of us what it is to be wearied and troubled, when matters went not to His comfort. 'The contradiction of sinners' covereth a great deal."

"I wonder," said Christie plaintively, "if He felt as if it hurt Him when His brethren banged the doors! Friswith alway does when she comes; and it is like as if she struck me on the ears. And she never seems to hear it!"

"I cannot tell, sweeting, what He felt in the days of His flesh at Nazareth; but I can tell thee a better thing—that He doth feel now, and for thee. 'I am poor and needy, but the Lord careth for me.' Keep that in thine heart, little Christie; it shall be like a soft pillow for thy weary head."

Alice rose to go home, and tied on her blue hood.

"O Aunt Alice, must you go? Couldn't you tarry till Father comes?"

"I think not, my dear heart. Tell thy father I had need to haste away, but I will come again and see both him and thee to-morrow."

To-morrow!

"Give him my loving commendations. Good-night, my child." And Alice hurried away.

Chapter Four.

Tabby shows her claws.

Friswith Hall was returning from Cranbrook in a state of great satisfaction. She had made an excellent bargain; and she was the sort of girl to whose mind a bargain had the flavour of a victory. In the first place, she had squeezed both coif and ribbon out of her money; and in the second, she had—as she fondly believed—purchased an article worth one-and-tenpence for eighteenpence.

As she came up to the last stile she had to pass, Friswith saw two girls sitting on it—the elder a slender, delicate-looking girl of some fourteen years, the younger a sturdy, little, rosy-faced damsel of seven. They looked up on hearing steps, and the elder quitted her seat to leave Friswith room to pass.

"Good-morrow, Pen! So you've got Patience there?"

"I haven't much, I'm afraid," said Pen, laughing. "I came out here because the lads made such a noise I could scarce hear myself speak; and I wanted to teach Patience her hymn. Charity knows hers; but Patience learns slower."

"Are they with you, then—both?"

"For a few days. Mistress Bradbridge is gone to visit her brother at Chelmsford, so she left her little maids with Mother."

"What a company must you be! How can you ever squeeze into the house?"

"Oh, folks can squeeze into small corners when they choose," said Penuel Pardue, with a smile. "A very little corner will hold both Charity and Patience."

"Then you haven't much of either," answered Friswith satirically. "Look you here, Pen!"

And unrolling her ribbon, she displayed its crimson beauties.

"What's that for?"

"For my hat! You can tell Beatrice, if you like, she won't be the best-dressed maid at church next Sunday."

"I should never suppose she would," was the quiet reply.

"Oh, I saw her blue ribbons! But I'll be as grand as she, you'll see now. Mother sent me to buy her a coif, and I got this for the money too. Don't you wish you were me?"

"No, Friswith, I don't think I do," said Penuel gravely.

"That's because you think Mother will scold. I'll stand up to her if she do. She's always bidding us stand up to folks, and I'll see how she likes it herself a bit!"

With which very dutiful speech, Friswith took her departure.

Penuel looked after her for a moment, and then, with a shake of her head which meant more than words, turned back to Patience and the hymn.

"Now, little Patience, try to learn the next verse. I will say it over to thee.

"'And in the presence of my foes

My table Thou shalt spread;

Thou shalt, O Lord, fill full my cup,

And eke anoint my head.'"

"Who be my foes, Pen?" said Patience.

"Folks that tease and trouble thee, my child."

"Oh!" responded Patience, instantly making a practical application. "Toby and Silas, that is. But they didn't see you spread the table, Pen. They were out playing on the green."

Penuel tried to "improve" this very literal rendering of the Psalm, but found it impossible to advance further than the awakening in Patience's mind an expectation of a future, but equally literal table, the dainties on which Toby and Silas would not be privileged to share.

"I won't give them the lessest bit, 'cause they're my foes," said Patience stubbornly. "You shall have some, Pen, and so shall Beatie—and Abbafull, if he's good. He tied my shoe."

"Aphabell, not Abbafull," corrected Penuel. "But, Patience, that won't serve: you've got to forgive your enemies."

"They shan't have one bit!" announced Patience, putting her hands behind her back, as if to emphasise her statement. "Pen, what does 'anoint my head' mean?"

"Pour oil on it," said Penuel.

"I won't have oil on my head! I'll pour it on Silas and Toby. It'll run down and dirt their clothes, and then Mother Pardue'll thwack 'em."

"Patience, Patience! Little maids mustn't want to have people thwacked."

"I may want my foes thwacked, and I will!" replied Patience sturdily.

"Look at the people coming up the road," answered Penuel, thinking it well to make a diversion. "Why, there's Master Benden and his mistress, and Mistress Hall, and ever so many more. What's ado, I marvel?"

About a dozen persons comprised the approaching group, which was brought up by a choice assortment of small boys, among whom Penuel's brothers, Esdras and Silvanus, were conspicuous. Mr Benden walked foremost, holding his wife by her wrist, as if he were afraid of her running away; whilst she went with him as quietly as if she had no such intention. Almost in a line with them was Tabitha Hall, and she was pouring out a torrent of words.

"And you'll rue it, Edward Benden, you take my word for it! You savage barbarian, to deal thus with a decent woman that never shamed you nor gave you an ill word! Lack-a-day, but I thank all the saints on my bended knees I'm not your wife! I'd—"

"So do I, Mistress!" was Mr Benden's grim answer.

"I'd make your life a burden to you, if I were! I'd learn you to ill-use a woman! I'd give it you, you white-livered dotipole (cowardly simpleton) of a Pharisee! Never since the world began—"

"Go to!" shrieked the boys behind, in great glee. "Scratch him, Tabby, do!"

Alice never uttered a word, either to her husband or her sister-in-law. She heard it all as though she heard not. Catching the eye of her brother Esdras, Penuel beckoned to him, and that promising youth somewhat reluctantly left the interesting group, and shambled up to his eldest sister at the stile.

"Esdras, what is all this? Do tell me."

"'Tis Master Benden, a-carrying of his mistress afore the Justices, and Mistress Hall's a-showing him the good love she bears him for it."

"Afore the Justices! Mistress Benden! Dear saints, but wherefore?"

"Oh, I wis nought of the inwards thereof," said Esdras, pulling a switch from the hedge. "Some saith one thing, and some another. But they saith she'll go to prison, safe sure."

"Oh, Esdras, I am sorry!" said Penuel, in a tone of great distress. "Mother will be sore troubled. Everybody loves Mistress Benden, and few loveth her master. There's some sorry blunder, be thou sure."

"Very like," said Esdras, turning to run off after the disappearing company.

"Esdras," said little Patience suddenly, "you've got a big hole in you."

"Oh, let be! my gear's alway in holes," was the careless answer. "It'll hold together till I get back, I reckon. Here goes!"

And away went Esdras, with two enormous holes in his stockings, and a long strip of his jacket flying behind him like a tail.

"Oh dear, this world!" sighed Penuel. "I'm afraid 'tis a bad place. Come, little Patience, let us go home."

When the girls reached Mrs Pardue's cottage, they found there the mother of Patience, Mrs Bradbridge. She sat talking earnestly to Mrs Pardue, who was busy washing, and said little in answer beyond such replies, compatible with business, as "Ay," "I reckon so," or "To be sure!"

"Mother!" said Penuel, as she led Patience in, "have you heard of this matter of Mistress Benden's?"

"Nay, child," replied Collet, stopping in the process of hanging up a skirt to dry. "Why, whatso? Naught ill, I do hope and trust, to Mistress Benden. I'd nigh as soon have aught hap evil to one of my own as her."

"Eh, neighbour, 'tis all a body need look for," sighed poor Widow Bradbridge, lifting Patience on her knee. "This world's naught save trouble and sorrow—never was sin' the Flood, more especially for women."

"She's had up to the Justices, Mother, but I couldn't hear for why; and her own husband is he that taketh her."

"He'll get his demerits, be sure," said Mrs Bradbridge.

"Well, and I wouldn't so much mind if he did," was Mrs Pardue's energetic comment. "He never was fit to black her shoes, he wasn't. Alice Benden afore the Justices! why, I'd as soon believe I ought to be there. If I'd ha' knowed, it should ha' cost me hot water but I'd ha' been with her, to cheer up and stand by the poor soul. Why, it should abhor any Christian man to hear of such doings!"

"Mistress Hall's withal, Mother: and I guess Master Benden 'll have his water served not much off the boil."

"I'm fain to hear it!" said Collet.

"Eh, she was at him, I can tell you! and she handled the matter shrewdly too. So was Esdras and Silas, and a sort more lads, a-crying, 'Scratch him, Tabby!' and she scraught him right well."

"The naughty caitiffs!" exclaimed their mother. "Howbeit, when they come home we shall maybe know the inwards of the matter."

The boys did not come home for some hours. When they did, Esdras slunk up the ladder, his garments being in a state which, as Silas had just kindly informed him, "smelt of the birch," and not desiring the application of that remedy sooner than could be helped. Silas flung his cap into the furthest corner, with a shout of "Hooray!" which sent his mother's hands to her ears.

"Bless the lad!—he'll deafen a body, sure enough! Now then, speak, caitiff, and tell us what's ado with Mistress Benden. Is she let off?"

"She's sent a-prison," shouted Silas, in tones which seemed likely to carry that information down the row. "Justice axed her why she went not to church, and quoth she, 'That can I not do, with a good conscience, since there is much idolatry committed against the glory of God.' And then she was committed. Justice didn't love his work o'er well, and Master Benden, as he was a-coming away, looked as sour as crabs. And old Tabby—Oh, lack-a-daisy-me! didn't she have at him! She's a good un, and no mistake! She stuck to his heels all the way along, and she beat him black and blue with her tongue, and he looked like a butt of alegar with a hogshead o' mustard in it. Hooray for old Tabby!"—and Silas announced that sentiment to the neighbourhood at the top of his very unsubdued voice.

Chapter Five.

Repentance.

"Sil-van-us Par-due!" Five very distinct syllables from his mother greeted the speech wherein Master Silas expressed his appreciation of the action of Mrs Tabitha Hall. "Silas, I would you were as 'shamed of yourself as I am of you."

"Well, Mother," responded Silas, with a twinkle in a pair of shining brown eyes, "if you'll run up yonder ladder and take half a look at Esdras, you'll not feel nigh so 'shamed of me at after!"

This skilful diversion of the attack from himself to his brother—a feat wherein every son of Adam is as clever as his forefather—effected the end which Master Silvanus had proposed to himself.

"Dear heart alive!" cried Mrs Pardue, in a flutter, "has that lad tore his self all o' pieces?"

"There isn't many pieces left of him," calmly observed Silas.

Mrs Pardue disappeared up the ladder, from which region presently came the sound of castigation, with its attendant howls from the sufferer, while Silas, having provided himself with a satisfactory cinder, proceeded, in defiance of Penuel's entreaties, to sketch a rather clever study of Mrs Tabitha Hall in the middle of his mother's newly washed table-cloth.

"Eh, Pen, you'll never do no good wi' no lads!" lamented Mrs Bradbridge, rising to depart. "Nought never does lads a bit o' good save thrashing 'em. I'm truly thankful mine's both maids. They're a sight o' trouble, lads be. Good even."

As Mistress Bradbridge went out, Mr Pardue was stepping in.

"Silas, let be!" said his father quietly; and Silas made a face, but pocketed the cinder for future use. "Pen, where's Mother?"

Mrs Pardue answered for herself by coming down the ladder.

"There! I've given it Esdras: now, Silas, 'tis thy turn."

No pussy cat could have worn an aspect of more exquisite meekness than Mr Silvanus Pardue at that moment, having dexterously twitched a towel so as to hide the work of art on which he had been engaged the moment before.

"I've done nothing, Mother," he demurely observed, adding with conscious virtue, "I never tear my clothes."

"You've made a pretty hole in your manners, my master," replied his mother. "Nicholas, what thinkest a lad to deserve that nicks Mistress Hall with the name of 'Old Tabby'?"

Nicholas Pardue made no answer in words, but silently withdrew the protecting towel, and disclosed the sufficiently accurate portrait of Mistress Tabitha on the table-cloth.

"Thou weary gear of a pert, mischievous losel!" (wretch, rascal) cried Collet. "Thou shalt dine with Duke Humphrey (a proverbial expression for fasting) this morrow, and sup on birch broth, as I'm a living woman! My clean-washed linen that I've been a-toiling o'er ever since three o' the clock! Was there nought else to spoil but that, thou rascal?"

"Oh ay, Mother," said Silas placidly. "There's your new partlet, and Pen's Sunday gown."

Mrs Pardue's hand came down not lightly upon Silas.

"I'll partlet thee, thou rogue! I'll learn thee to dirt clean gear, and make work for thy mother! If ever in all my born days I saw a worser lad—"

The door was darkened. Collet looked up, and beheld the parish priest. Her hold of Silas at once relaxed—a fact of which that lively gentleman was not slow to take advantage—and she dropped a courtesy, not very heartfelt, as the Reverend Philip Bastian made his way into the cottage. Nicholas gave a pull to his forelock, while Collet, bringing forward a chair, which she dusted with her apron, dismissed Penuel with a look.

The priest's face meant business. He sat down, leaned both hands on his gold-headed cane, and took a deliberate look at both Nicholas and Collet before he said a word beyond the bare "Good even." After waiting long enough to excite considerable uneasiness in their minds, he inquired in dulcet tones—

"What have you to say to me, my children?"

It was the woman who answered. "Please you. Father, we've nought to say, not in especial, without to hope you fare well this fine even."

"Indeed!—and how be you faring?"

"Right well, an't like you, Father, saving some few pains in my bones, such as I oft have of a washing-day."

"And how is it with thy soul, daughter?"

"I lack not your help therein, I thank you," said Collet somewhat spiritedly.

"Do you not so? I pray you, where have you stood in the church since last May, that never once have I, looking from the altar, seen your faces therein? Methinks you must have found new standing-room, behind the rood-screen, or maybe within the font," suggested the priest satirically. "Wit you that this is ever the beginning of heresy? Have you heard what has befallen your landlord's wife, Mistress Benden? Doubtless she thought her good name and repute should serve her in this case. Look you, they have not saved her. She lieth this night in Canterbury Gaol, whither you may come belike, an' you have not a care, and some of your neighbours with you. Moreover, your dues be not fully paid—"

"Sir," replied Nicholas Pardue, "I do knowledge myself behind in that matter, and under your good leave, I had waited on you ere the week were out. A labouring man, with a great store of children, hath not alway money to his hand when it most list him to pay the same."

"So far, well," answered the priest more amiably. "I will tarry a time, trusting you shall in other ways return to your duty. God give you a good even!"

And with seven shillings more in his pocket than when he entered, the Rev. Philip Bastian went his way. Nicholas and Collet looked at each other with some concern.

"We've but barely 'scaped!" said the latter. "What do we now, Nick? Wilt go to church o' Sunday?"

"No," said Nicholas quietly.

"Shall I go without thee, to peace him like?"

"Not by my good-will thereto."

"Then what do we?"

"What we have hitherto done. Serve God, and keep ourselves from idols."

"Nick, I do by times marvel if it be any ill to go. *We* worship no idols, even though we bow down—"

"'Thou shalt not bow down to them' is the command."

"Ay, but they were images of false gods."

"Read the Commandment, good wife. They were 'any graven image, or the likeness of any thing that is in Heaven above, or in the earth beneath, or in the waters under the earth.' Not a word touching false gods read I there."

"Why, but that were to condemn all manner of painting and such like—even yon rogue's likeness of Mistress Hall yonder."

"Scarcely, methinks, so long as it were not made for worship. The cherubim were commanded to be made. But if so were, wife—whether were better, that the arts of painting and sculpture were forgotten, or that God should be dishonoured and His commands disobeyed?"

"Well, if you put it that way—"

"Isn't it the true way?"

"Ay, belike it is. But he'll be down on us, Nick."

"No manner of doubt, wife, but he will, and Satan too. But 'I am with thee, and no man shall invade thee to hurt thee,' (see Note) saith the Lord unto His servants."

"They've set on Mistress Benden, trow."

"Nay, not to hurt her. 'Some of you shall they cause to be put to death... yet shall not an hair of your head perish.'"

"Eh, Nick, how shall that be brought about?"

"I know not, Collet, neither do I care. The Lord's bound to bring it about, and He knows how. I haven't it to do."

"'Tis my belief," said Collet, shaking the table-cloth, in a fond endeavour to obliterate the signs of Master Silas and his art, "that Master Benden 'll have a pretty bill to pay, one o' these days!"

Her opinion would have been confirmed if she could have looked into the window at Briton's Mead, as Mr Benden's house was called. For Edward Benden was already coming to that conclusion. He sat in his lonely parlour, without a voice to break the stillness, after an uncomfortable supper sent up in the absence of the mistress by a girl whom Alice had not yet fully trained, and who, sympathising wholly with her, was not concerned to increase the comfort of her master. At that time the mistress of a house, unless very exalted, was always her own housekeeper and head cook.

Mr Benden was not a man usually given to excess, but he drank deeply that evening, to get out of the only company he had, that of his own self-reproachful thoughts. He had acted in haste—spurred on, not deterred, by Tabitha's bitter speeches; and he was now occupied in repenting considerably at leisure. He knew as well as any one could have told him, that he was an unpopular man in his neighbourhood, and that no one of his acquaintance would have done or suffered much for him, save that long-suffering wife who, by his own act, lay that night a prisoner in Canterbury Gaol. Even she did not love him—he had never given her room nor reason; but she would have done her duty by him, and he knew it.

He looked up to where her portrait hung upon the wall, taken ten years ago, in the bloom of her youth. The eyes were turned towards him, and the lips were half parted in a smile.

"Alice!" he said, as if the picture could have heard him. "Alice!"

But the portrait smiled on, and gave no answer.

"I'll have you forth, Alice," he murmured. "I'll see to it the first thing to-morrow. Well, not to-morrow, neither; market-day at Cranbrook. I meant to take the bay horse to sell there. Do no harm, trow, to let her tarry a two-three days or a week. I mean you no harm, Alice; only to bring you down a little, and make you submissive. You're a bit too much set on your own way, look you. I'll go to Master Horden and Master Colepeper, and win them to move Dick o' Dover to leave her go forth. It shall do her a power of good—just a few days. And I can ne'er put up with many suppers like this—I must have her forth. Should have thought o' that sooner, trow. Ay, Alice—I'll have you out!"

Note. Most of the Scriptural quotations are taken from Cranmer's Bible.

Chapter Six.

Peppered broth.

"Father! O Father! Must I forgive Uncle Edward? I don't see how I can."

"I'm afraid you must, Christie, if you look to follow Christ."

"But how can I? To use dear Aunt Alice so cruelly!"

"How can God forgive thee and me, Christie, that have used His blessed Son far, far worser than Uncle Edward hath used Aunt Alice, or ever could use her?"

"Father, have you forgiven him?"

It was a hard question. Next after his little Christie herself, the dearest thing in the world to Roger Hall was his sister Alice. He hesitated an instant.

"No, you haven't," said Christie, in a tone of satisfaction. "Then I'm sure I don't need if *you* haven't."

"Dost thou mean, then, to follow Roger Hall, instead of the Lord Jesus?"

Christie parried that difficult query by another.

"Father, *love* you Uncle Edward?"

"I am trying, Christie."

"I should think you'd have to try about a hundred million years!" said Christie. "I feel as if I should be as glad as could be, if a big bear would just come and eat him up!—or a great lion, I would not mind which it was, if it wouldn't leave the least bit of him."

"But if Christ died for Uncle Edward, my child?"

"I don't see how He could. I wouldn't."

"No, dear heart, I can well believe that. 'Scarce will any man die for a righteous man... But God setteth out His love toward us, seeing that while we were yet sinners, Christ died for us.' And He left us 'an ensample,' my Christie, 'that we should follow His steps.'"

"I can't, Father; I can't!"

"Surely thou canst not, without the Lord make thee able. Thou canst never follow Christ in thine own strength. But 'His strength is made perfect through weakness.' I know well, my dear heart, 'tis vastly harder to forgive them that inflict suffering on them we love dearly—far harder than when we be the sufferers ourselves. But God can enable us to do even that, Christie."

Christie's long sigh, as she turned on her cushion, said that it was almost too hard for her to believe. But before she had found an answer, the door opened, and Mrs Tabitha Hall appeared behind it.

"Well, Roger Hall, how love you your good brother-in-law this morrow?" was her greeting. "I love not his action in no wise, sister."

"What mean you by that? Can you set a man's action in one basket, and himself in another? It's a strain beyond E-la, that is." (See note.)

"We're trying to forgive Uncle Edward, Aunt," said Christie from her couch, in a rather lugubrious tone.

"Pleasant work, isn't it?" was Aunt Tabitha's answer. "I haven't forgiven him, nor tried neither; nor I amn't going."

"But Father says we must."

"Very good; let him set us the ensample."

Aunt Tabitha made herself comfortable in Mr Hall's big chair, which he vacated for her convenience. By her side she set down her large market-basket, covered with a clean cloth, from which at one end protruded the legs of two geese, and at the other the handle of a new frying-pan.

"I've been up to see him this morrow; I thought he'd best not come short o' bitters. But he's off to Cranbrook with his bay horse—at the least so saith Mall—and I shall need to tarry while he comes back. It'll not hurt: bitters never lose strength by standing. I'll have it out with him again, come this even."

"Best not, Tabitha. It should maybe turn to more bitters for poor Alice, if you anger him yet further. And we have no right to interfere."

"What mean you by that, Roger Hall?" demanded Mistress Tabitha, in warlike tones. "No right, quotha! If that isn't a man, all o'er! I've a right to tell my brother-in-law he's an infamous rascal, and I'll do it, whether I have or no! No right, marry come up! Where else is he to hear it, prithee? You talk of forgiving him, forsooth, and Alice never stands up to him an inch, and as for that Tom o' mine, why, he can scarce look his own cat in the face. Deary weary me! where would you all be, I'd like to know, without I looked after you? You'd let yourselves be trod on and ground down into the dust, afore you'd do so much as squeal. That's not my way o' going on, and you'd best know it."

"Thank you, Sister Tabitha; I think I knew it before," said Mr Hall quietly.

"Please, Aunt Tabitha—" Christie stopped and flushed.

"Well, child, what's ado?"

"Please, Aunt, if you wouldn't!" suggested Christie lucidly. "You see, I've got to forgive Uncle Edward, and when you talk like that, it makes me boil up, and I can't."

"Boil up, then, and boil o'er," said Aunt Tabitha, half-amused. "I'll tarry to forgive him, at any rate, till he says he's sorry."

"But Father says God didn't wait till we were sorry, before the Lord Jesus died for us, Aunt Tabitha."

"You learn your gram'mer to suck eggs!" was the reply. "Well, if you're both in that mind, I'd best be off; I shall do no good with you." And Aunt Tabitha swung the heavy market-basket on her strong arm as lightly as if it were only a feather's weight. "Good-morrow; I trust you'll hear reason, Roger Hall, next time I see you. Did you sup your herbs, Christie, that I steeped for you?"

"Yes, Aunt, I thank you," said Christabel meekly, a vivid recollection of the unsavoury flavour of the dose coming over her, and creating a fervent hope that Aunt Tabitha would be satisfied without repeating it.

"Wormwood, and betony, and dandelion, and comfrey," said Aunt Tabitha. "Maybe, now, you'd best have a change; I'll lay some camomile and ginger to steep for you, with a pinch of balm—that'll be pleasant enough to sup."

Christabel devoutly hoped it would be better than the last, but she wisely refrained from saying so.

"As for Edward Benden, I'll mix him some wormwood and rue," resumed Aunt Tabitha grimly: "and I'll not put honey in it neither. Good-morrow. You've got to forgive him, you know: much good may it do you! It'll not do him much, without I mistake."

And Aunt Tabitha and her basket marched away. Looking from the window, Mr Hall descried Mr Benden coming up a side road on the bay horse, which he had evidently not succeeded in selling. He laughed to himself as he saw that Tabitha perceived the enemy approaching, and evidently prepared for combat. Mr Benden, apparently, did not see her till he was nearly close to her, when he at once spurred forward to get away, pursued by the vindictive

Tabitha, whose shrill voice was audible as she ran, though the words could not be heard. They were not, however, difficult to imagine. Of course the horse soon distanced the woman. Aunt Tabitha, with a shake of her head and another of her clenched fist at the retreating culprit, turned back for her basket, which she had set down on the bank to be rid of its weight in the pursuit.

Mr Benden's reflections were not so pleasant as they might have been, and they were no pleasanter for having received curt and cold welcome that morning from several of his acquaintances in Cranbrook. People manifestly disapproved of his recent action. There were many who sympathised but little with Alice Benden's opinions, and would even have been gratified by the detection and punishment of a heretic, who were notwithstanding disgusted and annoyed that a quiet, gentle, and generally respected gentlewoman should be denounced to the authorities by her own husband. He, of all men, should have shielded and screened her. Even Justice Roberts had nearly as much as told him so. Mr Benden felt himself a semi-martyr. The world was hard on disinterested virtue, and had no sympathy with self-denial. It is true, the world did not know his sufferings at the hands of Mary, who could not send up a decent hash—and who was privately of opinion that an improper hash, or no hash at all, was quite good enough for the man who had accused her dear mistress to the authorities. Mr Benden was growing tired of disinterested virtue, which was its own reward, and a very poor one.

"I can't stand this much longer; I must have Alice back!" was his reflection as he alighted from the bay horse.

But Nemesis had no intention of letting him off thus easily. Mistress Tabitha Hall had carried home her geese and frying-pan, and after roasting and eating the former with chestnut sauce, churning the week's supply of butter, setting the bread to rise, and indicating to Friswith and Joan, her elder daughters, what would be likely to happen to them if the last-named article were either over or under-baked, she changed her gown from a working woollen to an afternoon camlet, and took her way to Briton's Mead. Mr Benden had supped as best he might on a very tough chicken pie, with a crust not much softer than crockery, and neither his digestion nor his temper was in a happy condition, when Mary rapped at the door, and much to her own satisfaction informed her master that Mistress Hall would fain have speech of him. Mr Benden groaned almost audibly. Could he by an act of will have transported Tabitha to the further side of the Mountains of the Moon, nobody in Staplehurst would have seen much more of her that year. But, alas! he had to run the gauntlet of her comments on himself and his proceedings, which he well knew would not be complimentary. For a full hour they were closeted together. Mary, in the kitchen, could faintly hear their voices, and rejoiced to gather from the sound that, to use her own expression, "the master was supping his broth right well peppered." At last Mistress Tabitha marched forth, casting a Parthian dart behind her.

"See you do, Edward Benden, without you want another basin o' hot water; and I'll set the kettle on to boil this time, I promise you!"

"Good even, Mary," she added, as she came through the kitchen. "He (without any antecedent) has promised he'll do all he can to fetch her forth; and if he doesn't, and metely soon too, he'll wish he had, that's all!"

So saying, Mistress Tabitha marched home to inspect her bread, and if need were, to "set the kettle on" there also.

Note: *E-la* is the highest note in the musical system of Guido d'Aretino, which was popular in the sixteenth century. "A strain beyond E-la," therefore, signified something impossible or unreasonable.

Chapter Seven.

Wherein Alice comes home.

Partly moved by a faint sense of remorse, partly by Mrs Tabitha's sharp speeches, and partly also—perhaps most of all—by his private discomfort in respect of Mary's culinary unskilfulness, Mr Benden set himself to eat his dose of humble pie. He waited on Mr Horden of Finchcocks, and Mr Colepeper of Bedgebury Park, two of the chief men of position and influence in his neighbourhood, to entreat them to exert themselves in persuading the Bishop to release Alice as soon as possible. The diocese, of course, was that of Cardinal Pole; but this portion of it was at that time in the hands of his suffragan, Dr Richard Thornton, Bishop of Dover, whom the irreverent populace familiarly termed Dick of Dover. This right reverend gentleman was not of the quiet and reasonable type of Mr Justice Roberts. On the contrary, he had a keen scent for a heretic, and took great delight in bringing one into tribulation. On receiving the letters wherein Messrs Horden and Colepeper interceded for Alice Benden, his Lordship ordered the prisoner to be brought before him.

The Archbishop's gaoler went down to the prison, where Alice Benden, a gentlewoman by birth and education, shared one large room with women of the worst character and lowest type, some committed for slight offences, some for heavy crimes. These women were able to recognise in an instant that this prisoner was of a different order from themselves. Those who were not fallen into the depths, treated her with some respect; but the lowest either held aloof from her or jeered at her—mostly the latter. Alice took all meekly; did what she could for the one or two that were ailing, and the three or four who had babies with them; spoke words of Gospel truth and kindly sympathy to such as would let her speak them: and when sleep closed the eyes and quieted the tongues of most, meditated and communed with God. The gaoler opened the door a little way, and just put his head into the women's room. The prisoners might have been thankful that there were separate chambers for men and women... Such luxuries were unknown in many gaols at that date.

"Alice Benden!" he said gruffly.

Alice rose, gave back to its mother a baby she had been holding, and went towards the gaoler, who stood at the top of the stone steps which led down from the door.

"Here I am, Master Gaoler: what would you with me?"

"Tie on your hood and follow me; you are to come afore my Lord of Dover."

Alice's heart beat somewhat faster, as she took down her hood from one of the pegs around the room, and followed the gaoler through a long passage, up a flight of steps, across a courtyard, and into the hall where the Bishop was holding his Court. She said nothing which the gaoler could hear: but the God in whom Alice trusted heard an earnest cry of—"Lord, I am Thine; save Thine handmaid that trusteth in Thee!"

The gaoler led her forward to the end of a long table which stood before the Bishop, and announced her name to his Lordship.

"Alice Benden, of Briton's Mead, Staplehurst, an' it like your Lordship."

"Ah!" said his Lordship, in an amiable tone; "she it is touching whom I had letters. Come hither to me, I pray you, Mistress. Will you now go home, and go to church in time coming?"

That meant, would she consent to worship images, and to do reverence to the bread of the Lord's Supper as if Christ Himself were present? There was no going to church in those days without that. And that, as Alice Benden knew, was idolatry, forbidden by God in the First and Second Commandments.

"If I would have so done," she said in a quiet, modest tone, "I needed not have come hither."

"Wilt thou go home, and be shriven of thy parish priest?"

"No, I will not." Alice could not believe that a man could forgive sins. Only God could do that; and He did not need a man through whom to do it. The Lord Jesus was just as able to say to her from His throne above, as He had once said on earth to a poor, trembling, despised woman—"Thy sins be forgiven thee; go in peace."

Something had made "Dick of Dover" unusually gentle that afternoon. He only replied—"Well, go thy ways home, and go to church when thou wilt."

Alice made no answer. She was resolved to promise nothing. But a priest who stood by, whether mistakenly thinking that she spoke, or kind enough to wish to help her, answered for her—"She says she will, my Lord."

"Enough. Go thy ways!" said the Bishop, who seemed to wish to set her at liberty: perhaps he was a little afraid of the influential men who had interceded for her. Alice, thus dismissed, walked out of the hall a free woman. As she came out into Palace Street, a hand was laid upon her shoulder.

"Well, Alice!" said Edward Benden's voice. "I wrought hard to fetch you forth; I trust you be rightly thankful. Come home."

Not a word did he say of the pains he had taken originally to drive her into the prison; neither did Alice allude to that item. She only said in the meekest manner—"I thank you, Edward"—and followed her lord and master down Mercery Lane towards Wincheap Gate. She did not even ask whether he had made any preparations for her journey home, or whether he expected her to follow him on foot through the five-and-twenty miles which lay between Canterbury and Staplehurst. But when they reached the western corner of the lane, Mr Benden stopped at the old Chequers Inn, and in a stentorian voice demanded "that bay." The old bay horse which Alice knew so well, and which her husband had not succeeded in selling for more than its worth, as he desired, was brought forth, laden with a saddle and pillion, on the latter of which Alice took her place behind Mr Benden.

Not a word was spoken by either during the journey. They were about a mile from Staplehurst, and had just turned a corner in the road, when they were greeted by words in considerable number.

"Glad to see you!" said a brown hood—for the face inside it was not visible. "I reckoned you'd think better of it; but I'd got a good few bitters steeping for you, in case you mightn't. Well, Alice! how liked you yonder?—did Dick o' Dover use you metely well?—and how came he to let you go free? Have you promised him aught? He doesn't set folks at liberty, most commonly, without they do. Come, speak up, woman! and let's hear all about it."

"I have promised nothing," said Alice calmly; "nor am I like so to do. Wherefore the Bishop let me go free cannot I tell you; but I reckon that Edward here wist more of the inwards thereof than I. How go matters with you, Tabitha?"

"Oh, as to the inwards," said the brown hood, with a short, satirical laugh, "I guess I know as much as you or Edward either; 'twas rather the outwards I made inquiry touching. Me? Oh, I'm as well as common, and so be folks at home; I've given Friswith a fustigation, and tied up Joan to the bedpost, and told our Tom he'd best look out. He hasn't the spirit of a rabbit in him. I'd fain know where he and the childre 'd be this day month, without I kept matters going."

"How fares Christabel, I pray you?"

"Oh, same as aforetime; never grows no better, nor no worser. It caps me. She doesn't do a bit o' credit to my physicking—not a bit. And I've dosed her with betony, and camomile, and comfrey, and bugloss, and hart's tongue, and borage, and mugwort, and dandelion—and twenty herbs beside, for aught I know. It's right unthankful of her not to mend; but childre is that thoughtless! And Roger, he spoils the maid—never stands up to her a bit—gives in to every whim and fantasy she takes in her head. If she cried for the moon, he'd borrow every ladder in the parish and lash 'em together to get up."

"What 'd he set it against?" gruffly demanded Mr Benden, who had not uttered a word before.

"Well, if he set it against your conceit o' yourself, I guess he'd get high enough—a good bit higher than other folks' conceit of you. I marvel if you're ashamed of yourself, Edward Benden. I am."

"First time you ever were ashamed of yourself."

"Ashamed of *myself*?" demanded Tabitha Hall, in tones of supreme contempt, turning her face full upon the speaker. "You'll not butter your bread with that pot o' dripping, Edward Benden, if you please. You're not fit to black my shoes, let alone Alice's, and I'm right pleased for to tell you so."

"Good even, Mistress Hall; 'tis time we were at home."

"Got a home-truth more than you wanted, haven't you? Well, 'tis time enough Alice was, so go your ways; but as where 'tis time you were, my dainty master, that's the inside of Canterbury Gaol, or a worser place if I could find it; and you've got my best hopes of seeing you there one o' these days. Good den."

The bay horse was admonished to use its best endeavours to reach Briton's Mead without delay, and Mistress Tabitha, tongue and all, was left behind on the road.

"Eh, Mistress, but I'm fain to see you!" said Mary that evening, as she and Alice stood in the pleasant glow of the kitchen fire. "I've had a weary fortnight on't, with Master that contrarious, I couldn't do nought to suit him, and Mistress Hall a-coming day by day to serve him wi' vinegar and pepper. Saints give folks may be quiet now! We've had trouble enough to last us this bout."

"I am glad to come home, Mall," was the gentle answer. "But man is born to trouble, and I scarce think we have seen an end of ours. God learneth His servants by troubles."

"Well, I wouldn't mind some folks being learned thus, but I'd fain see other some have a holiday. What shall I dress for supper, Mistress? There's a pheasant and a couple of puffins, and a platter of curds and whey, and there's a sea-pie in the larder, and a bushel o' barberries."

"That shall serve, Mall. We had best lay in some baconed herrings for next fish-day; your master loves them."

"Afore I'd go thinking what he loved, if I were you!"

This last reflection on Mary's part was not allowed to be audible, but it was very earnest notwithstanding.

Chapter Eight.

Repenting his repentance.

It was Saturday evening, and three days after Alice returned home. Mr Benden sat in the chimney-corner, having just despatched a much more satisfactory supper than Mary had ever allowed him to see during her mistress's imprisonment; and Alice, her household duties finished for the day, came and sat in the opposite corner with her work.

The chimney-corner, at that date, was literally a chimney-corner. There were no grates, and the fire of logs blazed on a wide square hearth, around which, and inside the chimney, was a stone seat, comfortably cushioned, and of course extremely warm. This was the usual evening seat of the family, especially its elder and more honourable members. How they contrived to stand the very close quarters to the blazing logs, and how they managed never to set themselves on fire, must be left to the imagination.

Alice's work this evening was knitting. Stockings? Certainly not; the idea of knitted stockings had not yet dawned. Stockings were still, as they had been for centuries, cut out of woollen cloth, and sewn together like any other garment. The woman who was to immortalise her name by the brilliant invention of knitting stockings was then a little girl, just learning to use her needles. What Alice was knitting this evening was a soft woollen cap, intended for the comfort of Mr Benden's head.

The inside of the head in question was by no means so comfortable as Alice was preparing to make the outside. Mr Benden was pulled two ways, and not knowing which to go, he kept trying each in turn and retracing his steps. He wanted to make Alice behave herself; by which he meant, conform to the established religion as Queen Mary had Romanised it, and go silently to church without making insubordinate objections to idolatry, or unpleasant remarks afterwards. This was only to be attained, as it seemed to him, by sending her to prison. But, also, he wanted to keep her out of prison, and to ensure the continuance of those savoury suppers on which his comfort and contentment depended, and the existence of which appeared to depend on her remaining at home. How were the two to be harmoniously combined? Reflections of this kind resulted in making Mr Benden a very uncomfortable man; and he was a man with whom to be uncomfortable was to be unreasonable.

"Alice!" he said at last, after a period of silent thought Alice looked up from her work.

"The morrow shall be Sunday."

Alice assented to that indisputable fact.

"You'll come to church with me?"

For one instant Alice was silent. Her husband thought she was wavering in her decision, but on that point he was entirely mistaken. She was doing what Nehemiah did when he "prayed to the God of heaven" between the King's question and his answer. Well she knew that to reply in the negative might lead to reproach, prison, torture, even death. Yet that was the path of God's commandments, and no flowery By-path Meadow must tempt her to stray from it. In her heart she said to Him who had redeemed her—

> "Saviour, where'er Thy steps I see,
>
> Dauntless, untired, I follow Thee!"

and then she calmly answered aloud, "No, Edward, that I cannot do."

"What, hath your taste of the Bishop's prison not yet persuaded you?" returned he angrily.

"Nay, nor never will."

"Then you may look to go thither again, my mistress."

"Very well, Edward." Her heart sank low, but she did not let him see it.

"You'll either go to church, or here you bide by yourself."

"I thought to go and sit a while by Christie," she said.

"You'll not go out of this house. I'll have no whisperings betwixt you and those brethren of yours—always tuting in your ear, and setting you up to all manner of mischief. You'd not be so troublesome if you hadn't Roger Hall at your back—that's my belief. You may just keep away from them; and if they keep not away from you, they'll maybe get what they shall love little."

Alice was silent for a moment. Then she said very quietly, "As you will, Edward. I would only ask of you one favour—that I may speak once with Roger, to tell him your pleasure."

"I'll tell him fast enough when I see him. Nay, my mistress: you come not round me o' that fashion. I'll not have him and you plotting to win you away ere the catchpoll (constable) come to carry you hence. You'll tarry here, without you make up your mind to be conformable, and go to church."

The idea of escape from the toils drawing close around her had never entered Alice's brain till then. Now, for one moment, it surged in wild excitement through her mind. The next moment it was gone. A voice seemed to whisper to her—

"The cup which thy Father hath given thee, wilt thou not drink it?"

Then she said tranquilly, "Be it as you will. Because I cannot rightly obey you in one matter, I will be the more careful in all other to order me as you desire."

Mr Benden answered only by a sneer. He did not believe in meekness. In his estimation, women who pretended to be meek and submissive were only trying to beguile a man. In his heart he knew that this gentle obedience was not natural to Alice, who had a high spirit and plenty of fortitude; and instead of attributing it to the grace of God, which was its real source, he set it down to a desire to cheat him in some unrevealed fashion.

He went to church, and Alice stayed at home as she was bidden. Finding that she had done so, Mr Benden tried hard to discover that one of her brothers had been to see her, sharply and minutely questioning Mary on the subject.

"I told him nought," said Mary afterwards to Mistress Tabitha: "and good reason why—there was nought to tell. But if every man Jack of you had been here, do you think I'd ha' let on to the likes o' him?"

A very uncomfortable fortnight followed. Mr Benden was in the exasperating position of the Persian satraps, when they could find no occasion against this Daniel. He was angry with the Bishop for releasing Alice at his own request, angry with the neighbouring squires, who had promoted the release, angry with Roger Hall for not allowing himself to be found visiting his sister, most angry with Alice for giving him no reasonable cause for anger. The only person with whom he was not angry was his unreasonable self.

"If it wasn't for Mistress yonder, I should be in twenty minds not to tarry here," said Mary to Mistress Tabitha, whom she overtook in the road as both were coming home from market. "I'd as lief dwell in the house with a grizzly bear as him. How she can put up with him that meek as she do, caps me. Never gives him an ill word, no matter how many she gets; and I do ensure you, Mistress Hall, his mouth is nothing pleasant. And how do you all, I pray you? for it shall be a pleasure to my poor mistress to hear the same. Fares little Mistress Christabel any better?"

"Never a whit, Mall; and I am at my wits' end to know what I shall next do for her. She wearies for her Aunt Alice, and will not allow of me in her stead."

Mary felt privately but small astonishment at this.

"I sent Friswith and Justine over to tarry with her, but she seemed to have no list to keep them; they were somewhat too quick for her, I reckon." By quick, Mistress Hall meant lively. "I'll tell you what, Mary Banks—with all reverence I speak it, but I do think I could order this world better than it is."

"Think you so, Mistress Hall? And how would you go to do it?"

"First business, I'd be rid of that Edward Benden. Then I'd set Alice in her brother Roger's house, to look after him and Christabel. She'd be as happy as the day is long, might she dwell with them, and had that cantankerous dolt off her hands for good. Eh dear! but if Master Hall, my father-in-law, that made Alice's match with Benden, but had it to do o'er again, I reckon he'd think twice and thrice afore he gave her to that toad. The foolishness o' folks is beyond belief. Why, she might have had Master Barnaby Final, that was as decent a man as ever stepped in leather—he wanted her: but Benden promised a trifle better in way of money, and Master Hall, like an ass as he was, took up wi' him. There's no end to men's doltishness (foolishness). I'm homely, (plain-spoken) you'll say, and that's true; I love so to be. I never did care for dressing my words with all manner o' frippery, as if they were going to Court. 'Tis a deal the best to speak plain, and then folks know what you're after."

When that uncomfortable fortnight came to an uncomfortable end, Mr Benden went to church in a towering passion. He informed such of his friends as dared to approach him after mass, that the perversity and obduracy of his wife were beyond all endurance on his part. Stay another week in his house she should not! He would be incalculably indebted to any friend visiting Cranbrook, if he would inform the Justices of her wicked ways, so that she might be safely lodged again in gaol. An idle young man, more out of thoughtless mischief than from any worse motive, undertook the task.

When Alice Benden appeared the second time before the Bench, it was not with ease-loving, good-natured Justice Roberts that she had to do. Sir John Guildford was now the sitting magistrate, and he committed her to prison with short examination. But the constable, whether from pity or for some consideration of his own convenience, did not wish to take her; and the administration of justice being somewhat lax, she was ordered by that official to go home until he came for her.

"Go home, forsooth!" cried Mr Benden in angry tones. "I'll not have her at home!"

"Then you may carry her yourself to Canterbury," returned the constable. "I cannot go this week, and I have nobody to send."

"Give me a royal farthing, and I will!" was the savage answer.

The constable looked in his face to see if he meant it. Then he shook his head, dipped his hand into his purse, and pulled out half-a-crown, which he passed to Mr Benden, who pocketed this price of blood. Alice had walked on down the Market Place, and was out of hearing. Mr Benden strode after her, with the half-crown in his pocket.

Chapter Nine.

Alice decides for herself.

"Not that road, Mistress!"

Alice had nearly reached the end of the Market Place, when her husband's harsh call arrested her. She had been walking slowly on, so that he might overtake her. On hearing this, she paused and waited for him to come up.

"That's not the way to Canterbury!" said Mr Benden, seizing her by the wrist, and turning her round.

"I thought we were going home," said Alice quietly.

"Methinks, Mistress, there's somewhat wrong with your hearing this morrow. Heard you not the Justice commit you to gaol?"

"Truly I so did, Edward; but I heard also the constable to say that he would come for me when it should stand with his conveniency, and I reckoned it was thus settled."

"Then you reckoned without your host. The constable hath given me money to carry you thither without delay, and that will I with a very good will."

"Given you money!"

Through six years of unhappy married life Alice Benden had experienced enough of her husband's constant caprice and frequent brutality; but this new development of it astonished her. She had not supposed that he would descend so far as to take the price of innocent blood. The tone of her voice, not indignant, but simply astonished, increased Mr Benden's anger. The more gently she spoke, the harsher his voice grew. This is not unusual, when a man is engaged in wilfully doing what he knows to be wrong.

"Verily, your hearing must be evil this morrow, Mistress!" he said, with some wicked words to emphasise his remark. "The constable hath paid me a royal farthing, and here it is"—patting his pocket as he spoke—"and I have yet to earn it. Come, step out; we have no time to lose."

Alice came to a sudden stand-still.

"No, Edward," she said firmly. "You shall not carry me to gaol. I will have a care of your character, though you little regard mine. I pray you, unhand me, and I will go mine own self to the constable, and entreat him to take me, as his office and duty are." (This part of the story, however extraordinary, is pure fact.)

In sheer amazement, Mr Benden's hand unloosed from Alice's arm; and seizing her opportunity, she walked rapidly back to the Court House. For a moment he stood considering what to do. He had little more concern for his own reputation than for hers; but he felt that if he followed her to the constable, he could scarcely avoid refunding that half-crown, a thing he by no means desired to do. This reflection decided him. He went quickly to the inn where he had left his horse, mounted, and rode home, leaving Alice to her own devices, to walk home or get taken to Canterbury in any way she could.

The constable was not less astonished than Mr Benden. He was not accustomed to receive visits from people begging to be taken to gaol. He scratched his head, put it on one side and looked at Alice as if she were a curiosity in an exhibition, then took off his cap again, and scratched his head on the other side.

"Well, to be sure!" he said at last. "To tell truth, my mistress, I know not what to do with you. I cannot mine own self win this day to Canterbury, and I have no place to tarry you here; nor have I any to send withal save yon lad."

He pointed as he spoke to his son, a lad of about twelve years old, who sat on the bench by the Court House door, idly whistling, and throwing up a pebble to catch it again.

"Then, I pray you, Master Constable," said Alice eagerly, "send the lad with me. I am loth to put you to this labour, but verily I am forced to it; and methinks you may lightly guess I shall not run away from custody."

The constable laughed, but looked undecided.

"In very deed," said he, "I see not wherefore you should not go home and tarry there, till such time as I come to fetch you. But if it must be, it must. I will go saddle mine horse, and he shall carry you to Canterbury with George."

While the constable went to saddle the horse, and Alice sat on the bench waiting till it was ready, she fought with a very strong temptation. Her husband would not receive her, so much she knew for a certainty; but there were others who would. How welcome Roger would have made her! and what a perfect haven of rest it would be, to live even for a few days with him and Christabel! Her old father, too, at Frittenden, who had told her not many days before, with tears in his eyes, how bitterly he repented ever giving her to Edward Benden. It must be remembered that in those days girls were never permitted to choose for themselves, whether they wished to marry a man or not; the parents always decided that point, and sometimes, as in this instance, they came to a sadly mistaken decision. Alice had not chosen her husband, and he had never given her any reason to love him; but she had done her best to be a good wife, and even now she would not depart from it. The temptation was sore, and she almost gave way under it. But the constant habit of referring everything to God stood her in good stead in this emergency. To go and stay with her brother, whose visits to her Mr Benden had forbidden, would be sure to create a scandal, and to bring his name into even worse repute than it was at present. She must either be at Briton's Mead or in Canterbury Gaol; and just now the gaol was the only possible place for her. Be it so! God would go with her into the gaol—perhaps more certainly than into Roger's home. And the place where she could be sure of having God with her was the place where Alice chose and wished to be.

Her heart sank heavily as she heard the great door of the gaol clang to behind her. Alice was made of no materials more all-enduring than flesh and blood. She could enjoy rest and pleasantness quite as well as other people. And she wondered drearily, as she went down the steps into the women's room, how long she was to stay in that unrestful and unpleasant place.

"Why, are you come again?" said one of the prisoners, as Alice descended the steps. "What, you wouldn't conform? Well, no more would I."

Alice recognised the face of a decent-looking woman who had come in the same day that she was released, and in whom she had felt interested at the time from her quiet, tidy appearance, though she had no opportunity of speaking to her. She sat down now on the bench by her side.

"Are you here for the like cause, friend? I mind your face, methinks, though I spake not to you aforetime."

"Ay, we row in the same boat," said the woman with a pleasant smile, "and may as well make us known each to other. My name's Rachel Potkin, and I come from Chart Magna: I'm a widow, and without children left to me, for which I thank the Lord now, though I've fretted o'er it many a time. Strange, isn't it, we find it so hard to remember that He sees the end from the beginning, and so hard to believe that He is safe to do the best for us?"

"Ay, and yet not strange," said Alice with a sigh. "Life's weary work by times."

"It is so, my dear heart," answered Rachel, laying a sympathising hand on Alice's. "But, bethink you, He's gone through it. Well, and what's your name?"

"My name is Alice Benden, from Staplehurst."

"Are you a widow?"

Had Tabitha been asked that question in the same circumstances, she would not improbably have replied, "No; worse luck!" But Alice, as we have seen, was tender over her husband's reputation. She only returned a quiet negative. Rachel, whose eyes were keen, and ears ditto, heard something in the tone, and saw something in the eyes, which Alice had no idea was there to see and hear, that made her say to herself, "Ah, poor soul! he's a bad sort, not a doubt of it." Aloud she only said,—

"And how long look you to be here—have you any notion?"

Prisoners in our milder days are committed to prison for a certain term. In those days there was no fixed limit. A man never knew for a certainty, when he entered the prison, whether he would remain there for ten days or for fifty years. He could only guess from appearances how long it might be likely to be.

"Truly, friend, that know I not. God knoweth."

"Well said, Mistress Benden. Let us therefore give thanks, and take our hearts to us."

Just then the gaoler came up to them.

"Birds of a feather, eh?" said he, with not unkindly humour. For a gaoler, he was not a hard man. "Mistress Benden, your allowance is threepence by the day—what shall I fetch you?"

The prisoners were permitted to buy their own food through the prison officials, up to the value of their daily allowance. Alice considered a moment.

"A pennyworth of bread, an' it like you, Master; a farthing's worth of beef; a farthing's worth of eggs; and a pennyworth of ale. The halfpenny, under your good pleasure, I will keep in hand."

Does the reader exclaim, Was that the whole day's provision? Indeed it was, and a very fair day's provision too. For this money Alice would receive six rolls or small loaves of bread, a pound of beef, two eggs, and a pint of ale,—quite enough for supper and breakfast. The ale was not so much as it seems, for they drank ale at every meal, even breakfast, only invalids using milk. To drink water was thought a dreadful hardship, and they had no tea or coffee.

The gaoler nodded and departed.

"Look you, Mistress Benden," said Rachel Potkin, "I have thought by times to try, being here in this case, on how little I could live, so as to try mine endurance, and fit me so to do if need were. Shall we essay it together, think you? Say I well?"

"Very well, Mistress Potkin; I were fain to make the trial. How much is your allowance by the day?"

"The like of yours—threepence."

"We will try on how little we can keep in fair health," said Alice with a little laugh, "and save our money for time of more need. On what shall we do it, think you?"

"Why, I reckon we may look to do it on fourpence betwixt us."

"Oh, surely!" said Alice. "Threepence, I well-nigh think."

While this bargain was being made, Mr Benden sat down to supper, a pork pie standing before him, a dish of toasted cheese to follow, and a frothed tankard of ale at his elbow. Partly owing to her mistress's exhortations, Mary had changed her tactics, and now sought to mollify her master by giving him as good a supper as she knew how to serve. But Mr Benden was hard to please this evening. "The pork is as tough as leather," he declared; "the cheese is no better than sawdust, and the ale is flat as ditch-water." And he demanded of Mary, in rasping tones, if she expected such rubbish to agree with him?

"Ah!" said Mary to herself as she shut the door on him, "'tis your conscience, Master, as doesn't agree with you."

Chapter Ten.

Trying experiments.

Old Grandfather Hall had got a lift in a cart from Frittenden, and came to spend the day with Roger and Christabel. It was a holy-day, for which cause Roger was at home, for in those times a holy-day was always a holiday, and the natural result was that holiday-making soon took the place of keeping holy. Roger's leisure days were usually spent by the side of his little Christie.

"Eh, Hodge, my lad!" said Grandfather Hall, shaking his white head, as he sat leaning his hands upon his silver-headed staff, "but 'tis a strange dispensation this! Surely I never looked for such as this in mine old age. But 'tis my blame—I do right freely confess 'tis my blame. I reckoned I wrought for the best; I meant nought save my maid's happiness: but I see now I had better have been content with fewer of the good things of this life for the child, and have taken more thought for an husband that feared God. Surely I meant well,—yet I did evil; I see it now."

"Father," said Roger, with respectful affection, "I pray you, remember that God's strange dispensations be at times the best things He hath to give us, and that of our very blunders He can make ladders to lift us nearer to Himself."

"Ay, lad, thou hast the right; yet must I needs be sorry for my poor child, that suffereth for my blunder. Hodge, I would thou wouldst visit her."

"That will I, Father, no further than Saint Edmund's Day, the which you wot is next Tuesday. Shall I bear her any message from you?"

Old Mr Hall considered an instant; then he put his hand into his purse, and with trembling fingers pulled out a new shilling.

"Bear her this," said he; "and therewithal my blessing, and do her to wit that I am rarely troubled for her trouble. I cannot say more, lest it should seem to reflect upon her husband: but I would with all mine heart—"

"Well, Nell!" said a voice in the passage outside which everybody knew. "Your master's at home, I count, being a holy-day? The old master here likewise?—that's well. There, take my pattens, that's a good maid. I'll tarry a bit to cheer up the little mistress."

"Oh dear!" said Christabel in a whisper, "Aunt Tabitha won't cheer me a bit; she'll make me boil over. And I'm very near it now; I'm sure I must be singing! If she'd take me off and put me on the hob! Aunt Alice would, if it were she."

"Good-morrow!" said Aunt Tabitha's treble tones, which allowed no one else's voice to be heard at the same time. "Give you good-morrow, Father, and the like to thee, Christie. Well, Roger, I trust you're in a forgiving mood *this* morrow? You'll have to hammer at it a while, I reckon, afore you can make out that Edward Benden's an innocent cherub. I'd as lief wring that man's neck as eat my dinner!—and I mean to tell him so, too, afore I do it."

Aunt Tabitha left her sentence grammatically ambiguous, but practically lucid enough to convey a decided impression that a rod for Mr Benden was lying in tolerably sharp pickle.

"Daughter," said old Mr Hall, "methinks you have but a strange notion of forgiveness, if you count that it lieth in a man's persuading himself that the offender hath done him no wrong. To forgive as God forgiveth, is to feel and know the wrong to the full, and yet, notwithstanding the same, to pardon the offender."

"And in no wise to visit his wrong upon him? Nay, Father; that'd not a-pay me, I warrant you."

"That a man should escape the natural and temporal consequences of his evil doing, daughter, is not the way that God forgives. He rarely remits that penalty: more often he visits it to the full. But he loveth the offender through all, and seeks to purge away his iniquity and cleanse his soul."

"Well-a-day! I can fashion to love Edward Benden that way," said Tabitha, perversely misinterpreting her father-in-law's words. "I'll mix him a potion 'll help to cleanse his disorder, you'll see. Bitters be good for sick folks; and he's grievous sick. I met Mall a-coming; she saith he snapped her head right off yester-even."

"Oh dear!" said literal Christie. "Did she get it put on again, Aunt Tabitha, before you saw her?"

"It was there, same as common," replied Tabitha grimly.

"He's not a happy man, or I mistake greatly," remarked Roger Hall.

"He'll not be long, if I can win at him," announced Tabitha, more grimly still. "Good lack! there he is, this minute, crossing the Second Acre Close—see you him not? Nell, my pattens—quick! I'll have at him while I may!"

And Tabitha flew.

Christabel, who had lifted her head to watch the meeting, laid it down again upon her cushions with a sigh. "Aunt Tabitha wearies me, Father," she said, answering Roger's look of sympathetic concern, "She's like a blowy wind, that takes such a deal out of you. I wish she'd come at me a bit quieter. Father, don't you think the angels are very quiet folks? I couldn't think they'd come at me like Aunt Tabby."

"The angels obey the Lord, my Christie, and the Lord is very gentle. He 'knoweth our frame,' and 'remembereth that we are but dust.'"

"I don't feel much like dust," said Christie meditatively. "I feel more like strings that somebody had pulled tight till it hurt. But I do wish

Aunt Tabitha would obey the Lord too, Father. I can't think *she* knows our frame, unless hers is vastly unlike mine."

"I rather count it is, Christie," said Roger.

Mr Benden had come out for his airing in an unhappy frame of mind, and his interview with Tabitha sent him home in a worse. Could he by an effort of will have obliterated the whole of his recent performances, he would gladly have done it; but as this was impossible, he refused to confess himself in the wrong. He was not going to humble himself, he said gruffly—though there was nobody to hear him—to that spiteful cat Tabitha. As to Alice, he was at once very angry with her, and very much put out by her absence. It was all her fault, he said again. Why could she not behave herself at first, and come to church like a reasonable woman, and as everybody else did? If she had stood out for a new dress, or a velvet hood, he could have understood it; but these new-fangled nonsensical fancies nobody could understand. Who could by any possibility expect a sensible man to give in to such rubbish?

So Mr Benden reasoned himself into the belief that he was an ill-used martyr, Alice a most unreasonable woman, and Tabitha a wicked fury. Having no principles himself, that any one else should have them was both unnecessary and absurd in his eyes. He simply could not imagine the possibility of a woman caring so much for the precepts or the glory of God, that she was ready for their sakes to brave imprisonment, torture, or death.

Meanwhile Alice and her fellow-prisoner, Rachel Potkin, were engaged in trying their scheme of living on next to nothing. We must not forget that even poor people, at that time, lived much better than now, so far as eating is concerned. The Spanish noblemen who came over with Queen Mary's husband were greatly astonished to find the English peasants, as they said, "living in hovels, and faring like princes." The poorest then never contented themselves with plain fare, such as we think tea and bread, which are now nearly all that many poor people see from one year's end to another. Meat, eggs, butter, and much else were too cheap to make it necessary.

So Alice and Rachel arranged their provisions thus: every two days they sent for two pounds of mutton, which cost some days a farthing, and some a halfpenny; twelve little loaves of bread, at 2 pence; a pint and a half of claret, or a quart of ale, cost 2 pence more. The halfpenny, which was at times to spare, they spent on four eggs, a few rashers of bacon, or a roll of butter, the price of which was fourpence-halfpenny the gallon. Sometimes it went for salt, an expensive article at that time. Now and then they varied their diet from mutton to beef; but of this they could get only half the quantity for their halfpenny. On fish-days, then rigidly observed, of course they bought fish instead of meat. For a fortnight they kept up this practice, which to them seemed far more of a hardship than it would to us; they were accustomed to a number of elaborate dishes, with rich sauces, in most of which wine was used; and mere bread and meat, or even bread and butter, seemed very poor, rough eating. Perhaps, if our ancestors had been content with simpler cookery, their children in the present day would have had less trouble with doctors' bills.

Roger Hall visited his sister, as he had said, on Saint Edmund's Day, the sixteenth of November. He found her calm, and even cheerful, very much pleased with her father's message and gift, and concerned that Mary should follow her directions to make Mr Benden comfortable. That she forgave him she never said in words, but all her actions said it strongly. Roger had to curb his own feelings as he promised to take the message to this effect which Alice sent to Mary. But Alice could pretty well see through his face into his heart, and into Mary's too; and she looked up with a smile as she added a few words:—

"Tell Mall," she said, "that if she love me, and would have me yet again at home, methinks this were her wisest plan."

Roger nodded, and said no more.

Chapter Eleven.

Tabitha's basket.

Of all the persons concerned in our story at this juncture, the least unhappy was Alice Benden in Canterbury Gaol, and the most miserable was Edward Benden at Briton's Mead. His repentance was longer this time in coming, but his suffering and restlessness certainly were not so. He tried all sorts of ways to dispel them in vain. First, he attempted to lose himself in his library, for he was the rich possessor of twenty-six volumes, eight of which were romances of chivalry, wherein valiant knights did all kinds of impossibilities at the behest of fair damsels, rescued enchanted princesses, slew two-headed giants, or wandered for months over land and sea in quest of the Holy Grail, which few of them were sufficiently good even to see, and none to bring back to Arthur's Court. But Mr Benden found that the adventures of Sir Isumbras, or the woes of the Lady Blanchefleur, were quite incapable of making him forget the very disagreeable present. Then he tried rebuilding and newly furnishing a part of his house; but that proved even less potent to divert his thoughts than the books. Next he went into company, laughed and joked with empty-headed people, played games, sang, and amused himself in sundry ways, and came home at night, to feel more solitary and miserable than before. Then, in desperation, he sent for the barber to bleed him, for our forefathers had a curious idea that unless they were bled once or twice a year, especially in spring, they would never keep in good health. We perhaps owe some of our frequent poverty of blood to that fancy. The only result of this process was to make Mr Benden feel languid and weak, which was not likely to improve his spirits. Lastly, he went to church, and was shriven—namely, confessed his sins, and was absolved by the priest. He certainly ought to have been happy after that, but somehow the happiness would not come. He did not know what to do next.

All these performances had taken some time. Christmas came and passed—Christmas, with its morning mass and evening carols, its nightly waits, its mummers or masked itinerant actors, its music and dancing, its games and sports, its plum-porridge, mince-pies, and wassail-bowl. There were none of these things for Alice Benden in her prison, save a mince-pie, to which she treated herself and Rachel: and there might as well have been none for her husband, for he was unable to enjoy one of them. The frosts and snows of January nipped the blossoms, and hardened the roads, and made it difficult work for Roger Hall to get from Staplehurst to Canterbury: yet every holy-day his pleasant face appeared at the window of the gaol, and he held a short sympathising chat with Alice. The gaoler and the Bishop's officers came to know him well. It is a wonder, humanly speaking, that he was never arrested during these frequent visits: but God kept him.

"Good den, Alice," he said as he took leave of her on the evening of Saint Agnes' Day, the twenty-first of January. "I shall scarce, methinks, win hither again this month; but when our Lady Day next cometh, I will essay to see thee. Keep a good heart, my sister, and God be with thee."

"I do so, Roger," replied Alice cheerily. "Mistress Potkin here is a rare comfort unto me; and God is in Canterbury Gaol no less than at Staplehurst. I would fain, 'tis true, have been able to come and comfort Christie; but the Lord can send her a better help than mine. Give my loving commendations to the sweet heart, and may God reward thee for the brave comfort thou hast been to me all this winter! Farewell."

The next day, another and a less expected visitor presented himself. A tired bay horse drooped its weary head at the door of the Bishop's Palace, and a short, thick-set, black-haired man, with bushy eyebrows, inquired if he might be allowed to speak with his Lordship. The Bishop ordered him to be admitted.

"Well, and what would you, my son?" he asked condescendingly of the applicant.

"An't like your Lordship, my name is Edward Benden, of Staplehurst, and I do full reverently seek the release of my wife, that is in your gaol for heresy."

The Bishop shook his head. He had before now held more than one interview with Alice, and had found that neither promises nor threats had much weight with her. Very sternly he answered—"She is an obstinate heretic, and will not be reformed. I cannot deliver her."

"My Lord," responded Mr Benden, "she has a brother, Roger Hall, that resorteth unto her. If your Lordship could keep him from her, she would turn; for he comforteth her, giveth her money, and persuadeth her not to return."

"Well!" said the Bishop. "Go home, good son, and I will see what I can do." (This conversation is historical.)

If Mr Benden had not been in a brown study as he went into the Chequers to "sup his four-hours"—in modern phrase, to have his tea—and to give his horse a rest and feed before returning home, he would certainly have recognised two people who were seated in a dark corner of the inn kitchen, and had come there for the same purpose. The man kept his hat drawn over his face, and slunk close into the corner as though he were anxious not to be seen. The woman sat bolt upright, an enormous, full basket on the table at her right hand, and did not appear to care in the least whether she were seen or not.

"Is yon maid ever a-coming with the victuals?" she inquired in a rather harsh treble voice.

"Do hush, Tabby!" said the man in the most cautious of whispers. "Didst not see him a moment since?"

"Who? Dick o' Dover?"

"Tabitha!" was the answer in a voice of absolute agony. "Do, for mercy's sake!—Edward."

The last word was barely audible a yard away.

Mrs Hall turned round in the coolest manner, and gazed about till she caught sight of her brother-in-law, who happened to have his back to the corner in which they were seated, and was watching two men play at dominoes while he waited for his cakes and ale.

"Humph!" she said, turning back again. "Thomas Hall, I marvel if there be this even an hare in any turnip-field in Kent more 'feared of the hounds than you.—Well, Joan, thou hast ta'en thy time o'er these cakes."

The last remark was addressed to the waitress, who replied with an amused smile—

"An't like you, Mistress, my name's Kate."

"Well said, so thou bringest us some dainty cates (delicacies).—Now, Tom, help yourself, and pass that tankard."

"Tabitha, he'll hear!"

"Let him hear. I care not an almond if he hear every word I say. He'll hear o' t'other side his ears if he give us any trouble."

Mr Benden had heard the harsh treble voice, and knew it. But he was as comically anxious as Thomas Hall himself that he and the fair Tabitha should not cross each other's path that evening. To run away he felt to be an undignified proceeding, and if Tabitha had set her mind on speaking to him, utterly useless. Accordingly, he kept his back carefully turned to her, and professed an absorbing interest in the dominoes.

The cakes and ale having received due attention, Mr Hall paid the bill, and slunk out of the door, with the stealthy air and conscious face of a man engaged in the commission of a crime. Mrs Hall, on the contrary, took up her big basket with the open, leisurely aspect of virtue which had nothing to fear, and marched after her husband out of the Chequers.

"Now then, Thomas Hall, whither reckon you to be a-going?" she inquired, before she was down the steps of the inn, in a voice which must have penetrated much further than to the ears of Mr Benden in the kitchen. "Not that way, numskull!—to the left."

Poor Thomas, accustomed to these conjugal amenities, turned meekly round and trotted after his Tabitha, who with her big basket took the lead, and conducted him in a few minutes to the door of the gaol.

"Good den, Master Porter! We be some'at late for visitors, but needs must. Pray you, may we have speech of Mistress Benden, within here?"

The porter opened the wicket, and they stepped inside.

"You're nigh on closing time," said he. "Only half-an-hour to spare."

"I can do my business in half-an-hour, I thank you," replied Tabitha, marching across the courtyard.

The porter, following them, unlocked the outer door, and locked it again after them. To the gaoler who now received them they repeated their errand, and he produced another key, wherewith he let them into the women's prison. Alice and Rachel were talking together in the corner of the room, and Tabitha set down herself and her basket by the side of her sister-in-law.

"Good even, Alice!" she said, leaving her husband to see after himself, as she generally did. "We're a bit late, but better late than never, in especial when the ship carrieth a good cargo. Here have I brought you a couple of capons, a roll of butter, a jar of honey, and another of marmalade, a piece of a cheese, a goose-pie baken with lard, a pot o' green ginger, and nutmegs. I filled up with biscuits and reasons."

By which last word Mistress Tabitha meant to say that she had filled the interstices of her basket, not with intelligent motives, but with dried grapes.

"I con you right hearty thanks, Sister Tabitha," said Alice warmly, "for so rich provision! Verily, but it shall make a full pleasant change in our meagre diet; for my friend here, that hath been a mighty comfort unto me, must share in all my goods. 'Tis marvellous kindly in you to have thus laden yourself for our comforts. Good even, Tom! I am fain to behold thee. I trust you and all yours be well?"

"Maids lazy, Father 'plaining of pains in his bones, Christabel as is common, Roger well, Mary making o' candles," replied Tabitha rapidly. "As for yon ill-doing loon of a husband of yours, he's eating cakes and supping ale at the Chequers Inn."

"Edward here!" repeated Alice in surprised tones.

"Was when we came forth," said Tabitha, who while she talked was busy unlading her basket. "Hope your lockers 'll hold 'em. Time to close—good even! No room for chatter, Thomas Hall—say farewell, and march!"

And almost without allowing poor Thomas a moment to kiss his imprisoned sister, and beg her to "keep her heart up, and trust in the Lord," Mistress Tabitha swept him out of the door in front of her, and with the big basket on her arm, lightened of its savoury contents, marched him off to the Chequers for the horse.

Chapter Twelve.

Pandora.

In the projecting oriel window of a very pleasant sitting-room, whose inside seat was furnished with blue velvet cushions, sat a girl of seventeen years, dressed in velvet of the colour then known as lion-tawny, which was probably a light yellowish-brown. It was trimmed, or as she would have said, turned up, with satin of the same colour, was cut square, but high, at the throat, and finished by gold embroidery there and on the cuffs. A hood of dark blue satin covered her head, and came down over the shoulders, set round the front with small pearls in a golden frame shaped somewhat like a horseshoe. She was leaning her head upon one hand, and looking out of the window with dreamy eyes that evidently saw but little of the landscape, and thinking so intently that she never perceived the approach of another girl, a year or two her senior, and similarly attired, but with a very different expression in her lively, mischievous eyes. The hands of the latter came down on the shoulders of the meditative maiden so suddenly that she started and almost screamed. Then, looking up, a faint smile parted her lips, and the intent look left her eyes.

"Oh! is it you, Gertrude?"

"Dreaming, as usual, Pan? Confess now, that you wist not I was in the chamber."

"I scarce did, True." The eyes were growing grave and thoughtful again.

"Sweet my lady!—what conneth she, our Maiden Meditation? Doth she essay to find the philosopher's stone?—or be her thoughts of the true knight that is to bend low at her feet, and whisper unto her some day that he loveth none save her? I would give a broad shilling for the first letter of his name."

"You must give it, then, to some other than me. Nay, True; my fantasies be not of thy lively romancing sort. I was but thinking on a little maid that I saw yester-even, in our walk with Aunt Grena."

"What, that dainty little conceit that came up to the house with her basket of needlework that her mother had wrought for Aunt Grena? She was a pretty child, I allow."

"Oh no, not Patience Bradbridge. My little maid was elder than she, and lay on a day-bed within a compassed window. I marvelled who she were."

"Why, you surely mean that poor little whitefaced Christabel Hall! She's not pretty a whit—without it be her hair; she hath fair hair that is not over ill. But I marvel you should take a fantasy to her; there is nought taking about the child."

"You alway consider whether folks be pretty, Gertrude."

"Of course I do. So doth everybody."

"I don't."

"Oh, you! You are not everybody, Mistress Dorrie."

"No, I am but one maid. But I would fain be acquaint with that child. What said you were her name? All seems strange unto me, dwelling so long with Grandmother; I have to make acquaintance with all the folks when I return back home."

"Christabel Hall is her name; she is daughter to Roger Hall, the manager at our works, and he and she dwell alone; she hath no mother."

"No mother, hath she?—and very like none to mother her. Ah, now I conceive her looks."

"I marvel what you would be at, Pandora. Why, you and I have no mother, but I never mewled and moaned thereafter."

"No, Gertrude, I think you never did."

"Aunt Grena hath seen to all we lacked, hath not she?"

"Aunt is very kind, and I cast no doubt she hath seen to all you lacked." Pandora's tone was very quiet, with a faint pathos in it.

"Why, Dorrie, what lacked you that I did not?" responded Gertrude, turning her laughing face towards her sister.

"Nothing that I could tell you, True. What manner of man is this Roger Hall?"

"A right praisable man, Father saith, if it were not for one disorder in him, that he would fain see amended: and so being, Dorrie, I scarce think he shall be a-paid to have you much acquaint with his little maid, sithence he hath very like infected her with his foolish opinions."

"What, is he of the new learning?"

Gertrude failed to see the sudden light which shot into Pandora's eyes, as she dropped them on the cushion in the endeavour to smooth an entangled corner of the fringe.

"That, and no less. You may guess what Father and Aunt reckon thereof."

"Father was that himself, Gertrude, only five years gone, when I went to dwell in Lancashire."

"Pan, my dear heart, I do pray thee govern thy tongue. It maybe signifies but little what folks believe up in the wilds and forests yonder, and in especial amongst the witches: but bethink thee, we be here within a day's journey or twain of the Court, where every man's eyes and ears be all alive to see and hear news. What matters it what happed afore Noah went into the ark? We be all good Catholics now, at the least. And, Pan, we desire not to be burned; at all gates, I don't, if you do."

"Take your heart to you, sister; my tongue shall do you none ill. I can keep mine own counsel, and have ere now done the same."

"Then, if you be so discreet, you can maybe be trusted to make acquaintance with Christie. But suffer not her nor Roger to win you from the true Catholic faith."

"I think there is little fear," said Pandora quietly.

The two sisters were nieces of Mr Justice Roberts, and daughters of Mr Roberts of Primrose Croft, who was owner of the works of which Roger Hall was manager. Theirs was one of the aristocratic houses of the neighbourhood, and themselves a younger branch of an old county family which dated from the days of Henry the First. The head of that house, Mr Roberts of Glassenbury, would almost have thought it a condescension to accept a peerage. The room in which the girls sat was handsomely furnished according to the tastes of the time. A curtain of rich shot silk—"changeable sarcenet" was the name by which they knew it—screened off the window end of it at pleasure; a number of exceedingly stiff-looking chairs, the backs worked in tapestry, were ranged against the wall opposite the fire; a handsome chair upholstered in blue velvet stood near the fireplace. Velvet stools were here and there about the room, and cushions, some covered with velvet, some with crewel-work, were to be seen in profusion. They nearly covered the velvet settle, at one side of the fire, and they nestled in soft, plumy, inviting fashion, into the great Flanders chair on the other side. In one corner was "a chest of coffins"—be not dismayed, gentle reader! the startling phrase only meant half-a-dozen boxes, fitting inside each other in graduated sizes. Of course there was a cupboard, and equally of course the white-washed walls were hung with tapestry, wherein a green-kirtled Diana, with a ruff round her neck and a farthingale of sufficient breadth, drew a long arrow against a stately stag of ten, which, short of outraging the perspective, she could not possibly hit. A door now opened in the corner of the room, and admitted a lady of some forty years, tall and thin, and excessively upright, having apparently been more starched in her mind and carriage than in her dress. Pandora turned to her.

"Aunt Grena, will you give me leave to make me acquainted with Master Hall's little maid—he that manageth the cloth-works?"

Aunt Grena pursed up her lips and looked doubtful; but as that was her usual answer to any question which took her by surprise, it was not altogether disheartening.

"I will consult my brother," she said stiffly.

Mr Roberts, who was a little of the type of his brother the Justice, having been consulted, rather carelessly replied that he saw no reason why the maid should not amuse herself with the child if she wished it. Leave was accordingly granted. But Aunt Grena thought it necessary to add to it a formidable lecture, wherein Pandora was warned of all possible and impossible dangers that might accrue from the satisfaction of her desire, embellished with awful anecdotes of all manner of misfortunes which had happened to girls who wanted or obtained their own way.

"And methinks," concluded Mistress Grena, "that it were best I took you myself to Master Hall's house, there to see the maid, and make sure that she shall give you no harm."

Gertrude indulged herself in a laugh when her aunt had departed.

"Aunt Grena never can bear in mind," she said, "that you and I, Pan, are above six years old. Why, Christie Hall was a babe in the cradle when I was learning feather-stitch."

"Laugh not at Aunt Grena, True. She is the best friend we have, and the kindliest."

"Bless you, Dorrie! I mean her no ill, dear old soul! Only I believe she never was a young maid, and she thinks we never shall be. And I'll tell you, there was some mistake made in my being the elder of us. It should have been you, for you are the soberer by many a mile."

Pandora smiled. "I have dwelt with Grandmother five years," she said.

"Well, and haven't I dwelt with Aunt Grena well-nigh nineteen years? No, Pan, that's not the difference. It lieth in the nature of us two. I am a true Roberts, and you take after our mother's folks."

"Maybe so. Will you have with us, True, to Master Hall's?"

"I? Gramercy, no! I'm none so fond of sick childre."

"Christie is not sick, so to speak, Bridget saith; she is but lame and weak."

"Well, then she is sick, so *not* to speak! She alway lieth of a couch, and I'll go bail she whines and mewls enough o'er it."

"Nay, Bridget saith she is right full of cheer, and most patient, notwithstanding her maladies. And, True, the poor little maid is alone the whole day long, save on holy-days, when only her father can be with her. Wouldst thou not love well to bring some sunshine into her little life?"

"Did I not tell you a minute gone, Pandora Roberts, that you and I were cast in different moulds? No, my Minorite Sister, I should not love it—never a whit. I want my sunshine for mine own life—not to brighten sick maids and polish up poor childre. Go your ways, O best of Pandoras, and let me be. I'll try over the step of that new minuet while you are gone."

"And would you really enjoy that better than being kind to a sick child? O True, you do astonish me!"

"I should. I never was cut out for a Lady Bountiful. I could not do it, Dorrie—not for all the praises and blessings you expect to get."

"Gertrude, *did* you think—"

"An't like you, Mistress Pandora, the horses be at the door, and Mistress Grena is now full ready."

Chapter Thirteen.

A new friend for Christabel.

"O Aunt Tabitha! have you and Uncle Thomas been to Canterbury? and did you really see dear Aunt Alice? How looks she? and what said she? I do want to know, and Father never seems to see, somehow, the things I want. Of course I would not—he's the best father that ever was, Aunt Tabitha, and the dearest belike; but somehow, he seems not to *see* things—"

"He's a man," said Aunt Tabitha, cutting short Christabel's laboured explanation; "and men never do see, child. They haven't a bit of gumption, and none so much wit. Ay, we've been; but we were late, and hadn't time to tarry. Well, she looks white belike, as folks alway do when they be shut up from the air; but she seems in good health, and in good cheer enough. She was sat of the corner, hard by a woman that hath, said she, been a good friend unto her, and a right comfort, and who, said she, must needs have a share in all her good things."

"Oh, I'm glad she has a friend in that dreadful place! What's her name, Aunt, an' it like you?"

"Didn't say."

"But I would like to pray for her," said Christie with a disappointed look; "and I can't say, 'Bless that woman.'"

"Why not?" said Aunt Tabitha bluntly. "Art 'feared the Lord shall be perplexed to know which woman thou meanest, and go and bless the wrong one?"

"Why, no! He'll know, of course. And, please, has Aunt Alice a cushion for her back?"

Tabitha laughed curtly. "Cushions grow not in prisons, child. Nay, she's never a cushion."

"Oh, I'm sorry!" said Christie mournfully. "And I've got three! I wish I could give her one of mine."

"Well, I scarce reckon she'd have leave to keep it, child. Howbeit, thou canst pray thy father to make inquiration."

"Oh ay! I'll pray Father to ask. Thank you, Aunt Tabitha. Was Aunt Alice very, very pleased to see you?"

"Didn't ask her. She said some'at none so far off it. Dear heart! but what ado is here?"

And Tabitha rose to examine the details of the "ado." Two fine horses stood before the gate, each laden with saddle and pillion, the former holding a serving-man, and the latter a lady. From a third horse the rider, also a man-servant in livery, had alighted, and he was now coming to help the ladies down. They were handsomely dressed, in a style which showed them to be people of some consequence: for in those days the texture of a woman's hood, the number of her pearls, and the breadth of her lace and fur were carefully regulated by sumptuary laws, and woe betide the esquire's daughter, or the knight's wife, who presumed to poach on the widths reserved for a Baroness!

"Bless us! whoever be these?" inquired Tabitha of nobody in particular. "I know never a one of their faces. Have they dropped from the clouds?"

"Perhaps it's a mistake," suggested Christie.

"Verily, so I think," rejoined her aunt. "I'd best have gone myself to them—I'm feared Nell shall scarce—"

But Nell opened the door with the astonishing announcement of—"Mistress Grena Holland, and Mistress Pandora Roberts, to visit the little mistress."

If anything could have cowed or awed Tabitha Hall, it would certainly have been that vision of Mistress Grena, in her dress of dark blue velvet edged with black fur, and her tawny velvet hood with its gold-set pearl border. She recognised instinctively the presence of a woman whose individuality was almost equal to her own, with the education and bearing of a gentlewoman added to it. Christabel was astonished at the respectful way in which Aunt Tabitha rose and courtesied to the visitors, told them who she was, and that the master of the house was away at his daily duties.

"Ay," said Mistress Grena gently, "we wot that Master Hall must needs leave his little maid much alone, for my brother, Master Roberts of Primrose Croft, is owner of the works whereof he is manager."

This announcement brought a yet lower courtesy from Tabitha, who now realised that members of the family of Roger Hall's master had come to visit Christabel.

"And as young folks love well to converse together apart from their elders, and my niece's discretion may well be trusted," added Mistress Grena, "if it serve you, Mistress Hall, we will take our leave. Which road go you?"

"I will attend you, my mistress, any road, if that stand with your pleasure."

"In good sooth, I would gladly speak with you a little. I have an errand to Cranbrook, and if it answer with your conveniency, then shall you mount my niece's horse, and ride with me thither, I returning hither for her when mine occasion serveth."

Tabitha having intimated that she could make this arrangement very well suit her convenience, as she wished to go to Cranbrook some day that week, the elder women took their departure, and Pandora was left alone with Christie.

Some girls would have been very shy of one another in these circumstances, but these two were not thus troubled; Pandora, because she was too well accustomed to society, and Christie because she was too much excited by the unwonted circumstances. Pandora drew Christie out by a few short, well-directed questions; and many minutes had not passed before she knew much of the child's lonely life and often sorrowful fancies.

"Father's the best father that ever was, or ever could be!" said Christie lovingly: "but look you, Mistress, he is bound to leave me—he can't tarry with me. And I've no sisters, and no mother; and Aunt Tabitha can't be here often, and Aunt Alice is—away at present."

"Thou art somewhat like me, little Christie, for though I have one sister, I also have no mother."

"Do you miss her, Mistress?" asked Christie, struck by the pathos of Pandora's tone.

"Oh, so much!" The girl's eyes filled with tears.

"I can't remember my mother," said Christie simply. "She was good, everybody says; but I can't recollect her a whit. I was only a baby when she went to Heaven, to live with the Lord Jesus."

"Ah, but I do remember mine," was Pandora's answer. "My sister was thirteen, and I was eleven, when our mother died; and I fretted so much for her, they were feared I might go into a waste, and I was sent away for five years, to dwell with my grandmother, well-nigh all the length of England off. I have but now come home. So thou seest I can feel sorry for lonesome folks, little Christie."

Christie's face flushed slightly, and an eager, wistful look came into her eyes. She was nerving herself to make a confession that she had never made before, even to her father or her Aunt Alice. She did not pause to ask herself why she should choose Pandora as its recipient; she only felt it possible to say it to the one, and too hard to utter it to the others.

"It isn't only lonesomeness, and that isn't the worst, either. But everybody says that folks that love God ought to work for Him, and I can't do any work. It doth Him no good that I should work in coloured silks and wools, and the like; and I can't do nothing else: so I can't work for God. I would I could do something. I wouldn't care how hard it was. Justine—that's one of my cousins—grumbles because she says her work is so hard; but if I could work, I wouldn't grumble, however hard it was—if only it were work for God."

"Little Christie," said Pandora softly, stroking the fair hair, "shall I tell thee a secret?"

"If it please you, Mistress." The answer did not come with any eagerness; Christie thought the confession, which had cost her something, was to be shelved as a matter of no interest, and her disappointment showed itself in her face.

Pandora smiled. "When I was about thy years, Christie, one day as I came downstairs, I made a false step, and slid down to the bottom of the flight. It was not very far—maybe an half-dozen steps or more: but I fell with my ankle doubled under me, and for nigh a fortnight I could not walk for the pain. I had to lie all day on a day-bed; and though divers young folks were in the house, and many sports going, I could not share in any, but lay there and fretted me o'er my misfortune. I was not patient; I was very impatient. But there was in the house a good man, a friend of my grandmother, that came one even into the parlour where I lay, and found me in tears. He asked me no questions. He did but lay his hand upon my brow as I lay there with my kerchief to mine eyes, and quoth he, 'My child, to do the work of God is to do His will.' Hast thou yet learned my lesson, Christie?"

Christie's eyes were eager enough now. She saw that the answer was coming, not put aside for something more entertaining to Pandora.

"Many and many a time, Christie, hath that come back to me, when I have been called to do that which was unpleasing to me, that which perchance seemed lesser work for God than the thing which I was doing. And I have oft found that what I would have done instead thereof was not the work God set me, but the work I set myself."

"Then can I work for God, if I only lie here?"

"If God bid thee lie there, and bear pain and weakness, and weariness, dear child, then that is His work, because it is His will for thee. It would not be work for God, if thou wert to arise and scour the floor, when He bade thee 'bide still and suffer. Ah, Christie, we are all of us sore apt to make that blunder—to think that the work we set ourselves is the work God setteth us. And 'tis very oft He giveth us cross-training; the eager, active soul is set to lie and bear, while the timid, ease-loving nature is bidden to arise and do. But so long as it is His will, it is His work."

It did not strike Christie as anything peculiar or surprising that her new acquaintance should at once begin to talk to her in this strain. She had lived exclusively with people older than herself, and all whom she knew intimately were Christian people. Aunt Tabitha sometimes puzzled her; but Christie's nature was not one to fret and strain over a point which she could not comprehend. It seemed to her, therefore, not only right, but quite a matter of course, that Pandora Roberts should be of the same type as her father and her Aunt Alice.

"I thank you, Mistress," she said earnestly. "I will do mine utmost to bear it in mind, and then, maybe, I shall not be so impatient as oft I am."

"Art thou impatient, Christabel?"

"Oh, dreadfully!" said Christie, drawing a long sigh. "Not always, look you; there be times I am content, or if not, I can keep it all inside mostly. But there be times it will not tarry within, but comes right out, and then I'm so 'shamed of myself afterward. I marvel how it is that peevishness isn't like water and other things—when they come pouring out, they are out, and they are done; but the more peevishness comes out of you, the more there seems to be left in. 'Tis not oft, look you, it really comes right outside: that would be shocking! but 'tis a deal too often. And I *do* want to be like the Lord Jesus!"

Something bright and wet dropped on Christabel's forehead as Pandora stooped to kiss her.

"Little Christie," she said tenderly, "I too right earnestly desire to be like the Lord Jesus. But the best of all is that the Lord Himself desires it for us. He will help us both; and we will pray each for other."

Chapter Fourteen.

Unexpected tidings.

When Roger Hall came home that evening, he was greeted by Christie with an amount of excited enthusiasm which he did not often hear from his little invalid daughter.

"Oh Father, Father! I have a new friend, and such a good, pleasant maid she is!"

Christie did not term her new friend "nice," as she certainly would have done in the present day. To her ear that word had no meaning except that of particular and precise—the meaning which we still attach to its relative "nicety."

"A new friend, forsooth?" said Christie's father with a smile. "And who is she, sweet heart? Is it Mistress Final's niece, that came to visit her this last week?"

"Oh no, Father! 'Tis somebody much—ever so much grander! Only think, the master's daughter, Mistress Pandora Roberts, came with her aunt, Mistress Holland; and Mistress Holland went on to Cranbrook, and took Aunt Tabitha with her—she was here when she came—and Mistress Pandora tarried with me, and talked, till her aunt came back to fetch her. Oh, she is a sweet maid, and I do love her!"

Roger Hall looked rather grave. He had kept himself, and even more, his Christie, from the society of outsiders, for safety's sake. For either of them to be known as a Gospeller, the name then given to the true, firm-hearted Protestants, would be a dangerous thing for their liberties, if not their lives. Pandora Roberts was the daughter of a man who, once a Protestant, had conformed to the Romanised form of religion restored by Queen Mary, and her uncle was one of the magistrates on the Cranbrook bench. Roger was sorry to hear that one so nearly allied to these dangerous people had found his little violet under the leaves where he had hoped that she was safely hidden. A sharp pang shot through his heart as the dread possibility rose before him of his delicate little girl being carried away to share the comfortless prison of his sister. Such treatment would most likely kill her very soon. For himself he would have cared far less: but Christie!

He was puzzled how to answer Christie's praises of Pandora. He did not wish to throw cold water on the child's delight, nor to damage her newly found friend in her eyes. But neither did he wish to drag her into the thorny path wherein he had to walk himself—to hedge her round with perpetual cautions and fears and terrors, lest she should let slip some word that might be used to their hurt. An old verse says—

"Ye gentlemen of England

That sit at home at ease,

Ye little know the miseries

And dangers of the seas."

And it might be said with even greater truth—Ye men and women, ye boys and girls of free, peaceful, Protestant England, ye little know the dangers of life in lands where Popish priests rule, nor the miseries that you will have to endure if they ever gain the ascendancy here again!

Roger Hall had never heard Dr Abernethy's wise advice—"When you don't know what to do, do nothing." But in this emergency he acted on that principle.

"I trust, my dear heart," he said quietly, "that it may please the Lord to make thee and this young gentlewoman a blessing to each other."

"Oh, it will, I know, Father!" said Christie, quite unsuspicious of the course of her father's thoughts. "Only think, Father! she told me first thing, pretty nigh, that she loved the Lord Jesus, and wanted to be like Him. So you see we couldn't do each other any hurt, could we?"

Roger smiled rather sadly.

"I am scarce so sure of that, my Christie. Satan can set snares even for them that love the Lord; but 'tis true, they be not so like to slip as they that do not. Is this young mistress she that dwelt away from home some years back, or no?"

"She is, Father; she hath dwelt away in the shires, with her grandmother, these five years. And there was a good man there—she told me not his name—that gave her counsel, and he said, 'To do God's work is to do God's will.' That is good, Father, isn't it?"

"Good, and very true, sweeting."

Roger Hall had naturally all the contempt of a trueborn man of Kent for the dwellers in "the shires," which practically meant everybody in England who was not a native of Kent. But he knew that God had said, "He that despiseth his neighbour sinneth;" so he said in his heart, "Get thee behind me, Satan," to the bad feeling, and went on to wonder who the good man might be. Had Pandora told the name of that man, half Roger's doubts and terrors would have taken flight. The name of Master John Bradford of Manchester—the martyr who eighteen months before had glorified the Lord in the fires—would have been an immediate passport to his confidence. But Pandora knew the danger of saying more than was needful, and silently suppressed the name of her good counsellor.

Some days elapsed before Roger was again able to visit Canterbury. They were very busy just then at the cloth-works, and his constant presence was required. But when February began, the pressure was past, and on the first holy-day in that month, which was Candlemas Day, he rode to the metropolitan city of his county on another visit to Alice. On his arm he carried a basket, which held a bottle of thick cream, a dozen new-laid eggs, and a roll of butter; and as he came through Canterbury, he added to these country luxuries the town dainties of a bag of dates and half a pound each of those costly spices, much used and liked at that time—cloves, nutmeg, and cinnamon. On these articles he spent 7 shillings 8 pence—8 pence for the dates, 3 shillings for cinnamon, 2 shillings 6 pence for cloves, and 1 shilling 6 pence for nutmegs. Lastly, he bought a sugarloaf, then an unusual luxury, which cost him 7 pence. The basket was now quite full, and leaving his horse at the Star Inn, he went up to the prison, and struck with his dagger on the great bell, which was then the general mode of ringing it. Every man, except labourers, carried a dagger. The porter had become so accustomed to the sight of Roger, that he usually opened the door for him at once, with a nod of greeting. But this morning, when he looked from the wicket to see who it was, he did not open the door, but stood silently behind it. Roger wondered what this new style of conduct meant.

"May I within, by your good leave, to see my sister?" he asked.

"You may within, if you desire to tarry here, by my Lord's good leave," said the porter; "but you'll not see your sister."

"Why, what's ado?" asked Roger in consternation.

"Removed," answered the porter shortly.

"Whither?"

"Ask me no questions, and I'll tell you no lies," was the proverbial reply.

"Lack-a-day! Can I find out?"

The porter elevated his eyebrows, and shrugged his shoulders.

"Come within a moment," said he.

Roger obeyed, and the porter drew him into his lodge, where he spoke in a cautious whisper.

"Master Hall, you be an honest man; and though I am here found, yet I trust so am I. If you be likewise a wise man, you will find somewhat to keep you at home for the future. Whither Mistress Benden is now taken, I could not tell you if I would: but this can I say, you'll follow if you have not a care. Be ruled by me, that am dealing by you as by a friend, and keep out of Canterbury when you are out, and let that be as soon as you may. For your good stuff, leave it an' you will for Mistress Potkin: but if you tarry here, or return and be taken, say not you were not warned. Now, void your basket, and go."

Like a man dazed or in a dream, Roger Hall slowly emptied his basket of the good things which he had brought for Alice. He was willing enough that Rachel Potkin should have those or any other comforts he could bring her. But that basket had been packed under Christie's eyes, and in part by Christie's hands, and the child had delighted herself in the thought of Aunt Alice's pleasure in every item. And when at last the roll of butter was lifted out, and behind it the eggs which it had confined in a safe corner, and Roger came to the two tiny eggs which Christie had put in with special care, saying, "Now, Father, you'll be sure to tell Aunt Alice those eggs were laid by my own little hen, and she must eat them her own self, because I sent them to her"—as Roger took out the eggs of Christie's hen, he could hardly restrain a sob, which was partly for the child's coming disappointment, and partly caused by his own anxious suspense and distress. The porter had not spoken very plainly—he had probably avoided doing so on purpose—but it was sufficiently manifest that the authorities had their eyes on Roger himself, and that he ran serious risk of arrest if he remained in Canterbury.

But what had they done with Alice? He must find her. Whatever became of him, he must look for Alice.

Roger turned away from the gate of the gaol, sick at heart. He scarcely remembered even to thank the friendly porter, and turned back to repair the omission.

"If you be thankful to me," was the porter's significant answer, "look you take my counsel."

Slowly, as if he were walking in a dream, and scarcely knew where he was going, Roger made his way back to the Star. There all was bustle and commotion, for some people of high rank had just arrived on a pilgrimage to the shrine of Saint Thomas of Canterbury, or rather to the place where the shrine had stood in past ages. King Henry the Eighth had destroyed the shrine, and a soldier had "rattled down proud Becket's glassy bones," but the spot where it had been was considered holy, and the poor deluded people even yet sometimes came to worship there, and to make their painful way up the Pilgrims' Stairs, which they had to ascend on their knees. Those stairs are now to be seen in Canterbury Cathedral, worn by the thousands of knees which went up them, the poor creatures fancying that by this means they would obtain pardon of their sins, or earn a seat in Heaven.

The bustle in the inn rather favoured Roger's escape. He mounted his horse, tied the basket to his saddle, and rode out of Wincheap Gate, wondering all the while how he could discover the place to which Alice had been removed, and how he should tell Christie. He met several people on the road, but noticed none of them, and reached his own house without having exchanged a word with any one he knew. He let himself in, and with a sinking heart, opened the parlour door.

"Dear heart, Master Hall!" said the voice of Collet Pardue, who was seated by Christie's couch, "but there's ill news in your face! What's ado, prithee?"

"Oh, Father, is Aunt Alice sick?" cried Christie.

Roger came round to the couch, and knelt down, one hand clasping that of his little girl, and the other tenderly laid upon her head.

"My Christie," he said, "they have taken Aunt Alice away, I know not whither. But our Father knows. Perchance He will show us. But whether or not, all is well with her, for she is in His care that loveth her more than we."

Chapter Fifteen.

Mr Benden's dessert.

"Taken her away from the gaol! and you wot not whither? Well, Roger Hall, you're as pretty a man of your hands as ever I did behold!"

"How signify you, Sister Tabitha?"

"Would I ever have turned back from Canterbury till I'd found out? Marry, not I! I'd have known all about it in half a twink."

"Please, Aunt Tabitha, if you have half a twink to spare—I know not what it is, but I suppose you do—won't you go and find out Aunt Alice?"

This practical suggestion from Christie was quietly ignored.

"'Tis right like a man as ever I did see! Catch a woman turning back in that fashion afore she'd half done her work!"

"But, Aunt Tabitha," urged Christie, for her father sat in silence, and she felt herself bound to defend him, "have you forgotten what the porter said to Father? If they—"

"Pack o' nonsense!" snorted Aunt Tabitha. "He would fain keep him from continual coming, and he spake out the first thing that came in his head, that's all. None but a babe like thee should take any note of such rubbish. Can't you speak up, Roger Hall? or did you drop your tongue where you left your wits?"

"Methinks you have a sufficiency for us both, Tabitha," said Roger quietly, leaving it uncertain whether he alluded to the tongue or the wits.

"Mean you to go again to-morrow?"

"That cannot I yet say. I lack time to think—and to pray likewise."

"Lack time to *think*! Gramercy me! How long doth a man want to gather up his wits together? I should have thought of fifty things whilst I rode back from Canterbury."

"So I did, Tabitha; but I wis not yet which was the right."

"Ay, you're a brave hand at thinking, but I want to *do*."

"That will I likewise, so soon as I have thought out what is best to do. I see it not as yet."

"Lack-a-daisy me! Well, my fine master, I'll leave you to your thinking, and I'll get to my doing. As to second and third, I'll tarry till I reach 'em; but I know what comes first."

"What mean you to do, Tabitha?"

"I mean to walk up to Briton's Mead, and give Edward Benden a sweet-sop to his supper. I've had a rod in pickle any day this three months, and I reckon 'tis in good conditions by now. I'll give him some'at he'll enjoy. If he skrike not afore I've done with him—!"

Leaving her sentence the more expressive for its incompleteness, Mistress Tabitha stalked out of the room and the house, not pausing for any farewells.

"Father," said Christie, a little fearfully, "aren't you 'feared Aunt Tabitha shall get into prison, the way she talks and runs right at things?"

"Nay, Christie, I scarce am," said Roger.

He knew that Faithful is brought to the stake in Vanity Fair more frequently than Talkative.

In the dining-room at Briton's Mead Mr Benden was sitting down to his solitary supper. Of the result of his application to the Bishop he had not yet heard. He really imagined that if Roger Hall could be kept out of her way, Alice would yield and do all that he wished. He gave her credit for no principle; indeed, like many in his day, he would have laughed at the bare idea of a woman having any principle, or being able to stand calmly and firmly without being instigated and supported by a man. Roger, therefore, in his eyes, was the obstacle in the way of Alice's submission. He did not in the least realise that the real obstacle against which he was striving was the Holy Spirit of God.

To a man in Mr Benden's position, who, moreover, had always been an epicure, his meals were a relief and an enjoyment. He was then less troubled by noxious thoughts than at any other time. It was with a sigh of something like satisfaction that he sat down to supper, unfolded his napkin, and tucked it into his doublet, muttered a hurried grace, and helped himself to the buttered eggs which Mary had sent up light and hot. He was just putting down the pepper-cruet, when he became aware of something on the settle in the corner, which he could not fairly see, and did not understand. Mr Benden was rather short-sighted. He peered with eyes half shut at the unknown object.

"What's that?" he said, half aloud.

That responded by neither sound nor motion. It looked very like a human being; but who could possibly be seated on his settle at this late hour without his knowing it? Mr Benden came to the conclusion that it would be foolish to disturb himself, and spoil an excellent supper, for the sake of ascertaining that Mary had forgotten to put away his fur-lined cloak, which was most likely the thing in the corner. He would look at it after supper. He took up his spoon, and was in the act of conveying it to his mouth, when the uncanny object suddenly changed its attitude.

"Saints bless us and love us!" ejaculated Mr Benden, dropping the spoon.

He really was not at all concerned about the saints loving him, otherwise he would have behaved differently to his wife; but the words were the first to occur to him. The unknown thing was still again, and after another long stare, which brought him no information, Mr Benden picked up the spoon, and this time succeeded in conveying it to his lips.

At that moment the apparition spoke.

"Edward Benden!" it said, "do you call yourself a Christian?"

Mr Benden's first gasp of horror that the hobgoblin should address him by name, was succeeded by a second of relief as he recognised the voice.

"Bless the saints!" he said to himself; "it's only Tabby."

His next sensation was one of resentment. What business had Tabitha to steal into his house in this way, startling him half out of his wits as he began his supper? These mixed sentiments lent a sulky tone to his voice as he answered that he was under the impression he had some claim to that character.

"Because," said the apparition coolly, "I don't."

"Never thought you were," said Mr Benden grimly, turning the tables on the enemy, who had left him a chance to do it.

Tabitha rose and advanced to the table.

"Where is Alice?" she demanded.

"How should I know?" answered Mr Benden, hastily shovelling into his mouth another spoonful of eggs, without a notion what they tasted like. "In the gaol, I reckon. You are best to go and see, if you'd fain know. I'm not her keeper."

"You're not? Did I not hear you swear an oath to God Almighty, to 'keep her in sickness and in health?' That's how you keep your vows, is it? I've kept mine better than so. But being thus ignorant of what you should know better than other folks, may be it shall serve you to hear that she is not in the gaol, nor none wist where she is, saving, as I guess, yon dotipole men call Dick o' Dover. He and Satan know, very like, for I count they took counsel about it."

Mr Benden laid down his spoon, and looked up at Tabitha. "Tabitha, I wist nought of this, I ensure you, neither heard I of it aforetime. I—"

He took another mouthful to stop the words that were coming. It would hardly be wise to let Tabitha know what he had said to the Bishop.

"Sit you down, and give me leave to help you to these eggs," he said, hospitably in appearance, politically in fact.

"I'll not eat nor drink in your house," was the stern reply. "Must I, then, take it that Dick o' Dover hath acted of his own head, and without any incitement from you?"

Poor Mr Benden! He felt himself fairly caught. He did not quite want to tell a point blank falsehood.

"They be good eggs, Tabitha, and Mall wist well how to dress them," he urged. "You were best—"

"You were best answer my question, Edward Benden: Did you in any wise excite yon mitred scoundrel to this act?"

"Your language, Tabitha, doth verily 'shame me. 'Mitred scoundrel,' in good sooth! Fear you not to be brought afore the justices for—"

"I fear nought so much as I fear you are a slippery snake, as well as a roaring lion," said Tabitha, in grim defiance of natural history. "Answer my question, or I'll make you!"

Until that moment Mr Benden had not noticed that Tabitha kept one hand behind her. It suddenly struck him now, in disagreeable combination with the threat she uttered.

"What have you behind your back?" he said uneasily.

"A succade to follow your eggs, which you shall have if you demerit it."

"What mean you, Sister Tabitha?"

"Let be your slimy coaxing ways. Answer my question."

Like all bullies, Mr Benden was a coward. With a woman of Tabitha's type he had never before had to deal at such close quarters. Alice either yielded to his wishes, or stood quietly firm, and generally silent. He began to feel considerable alarm. Tabitha was a powerful woman, and he was a man of only moderate strength. Briton's Mead was not within call of any other house, and its master had an unpleasant conviction that to summon Mary to his aid would not improve his case. It was desirable to compromise with Tabitha. The only way that he could see to do it was to deny his action. If he did commit a sin in speaking falsely, he said to himself, it was Tabitha's fault for forcing him to it, and Father Bastian would absolve him easily, considering the circumstances.

"No, Tabitha; I did not say a word to the Bishop."

"You expect me to believe you, after all that fencing and skulking under hedges? Then I don't. If you'd said it fair out at first, well—may be I might, may be I mightn't. But I don't now, never a whit. And I think you'd best eat the succade I brought you. I believe you demerit it; and if you don't, you soon will, or I'm a mistaken woman, and I'm not apt to be that," concluded Mistress Tabitha, with serene consciousness of virtue.

"Tabitha, my dear sister, I do ensure you—"

"You'd best ensure me of nothing, my right undear brother. Out on your snaky speeches and beguiling ways! You'll have your succade, and I'll leave you to digest it, and much good may it do you!"

And he had it. After which transaction Mistress Tabitha went home, and slept all the better for the pleasing remembrance that she had horsewhipped Mr Edward Benden.

Chapter Sixteen.

At the White Hart.

There was a good deal of bustle going on in the kitchen of the White Hart, the little hostelry at Staplehurst. It was "fair day," and fairs were much more important things in the olden time than now. A fair now-a-days is an assemblage of some dozen booths, where the chief commodities are toys and sweetmeats, with an attempt at serious business in the shape of a little crockery or a few tin goods. But fairs in 1557 were busy places where many people laid in provisions for the season, or set themselves up with new clothes. The tiny inn had as many guests as it could hold, and the principal people in the town had come together in its kitchen—country inns had no parlours then—to debate all manner of subjects in which they were interested. The price of wool was an absorbing topic with many; the dearness of meat and general badness of trade were freely discussed by all. Amongst them bustled Mistress Final, the landlady of the inn, a widow, and a comely, rosy-faced, fat, kindly woman, assisted by her young son Ralph, her two daughters, Ursula and Susan, and her maid Dorcas. Cakes and ale were served to most of the customers; more rarely meat, except in the form of pies, which were popular, or of bacon, with or without accompanying eggs.

The company in the kitchen were all more or less acquainted with each other, two persons excepted. Those who were not Staplehurst people had come in from the surrounding villages, or from Cranbrook at the farthest. But these two men were total strangers, and they did not mix with the villagers, but sat, in travelling garb, at one corner of the kitchen, listening, yet rarely joining in the talk which went on around them. One of them, indeed, seemed wrapped in his own thoughts, and scarcely spoke, even to his companion. He was a tall spare man, with a grave and reserved expression of countenance. The other was shorter and much more lively in his motions, was evidently amused by the conversation in his vicinity, and looked as if he would not object to talk if the opportunity were given him.

Into this company came Emmet Wilson and Collet Pardue. Both had brought full baskets from the fair, which they set down in a corner, and turned to amuse themselves with a little chat with their friends.

"Any news abroad?" asked Collet. She dearly loved a bit of news, which she would retail to her quiet husband as they sat by the fireside after the day's work was done.

"Well, not so much," said John Banks, the mason, to whom Collet had addressed herself. He was the brother of Mr Benden's servant Mary. "Without you call it news to hear what happed at Briton's Mead last night."

"Why, whatso? Not the mistress come home, trow?"

"Alack, no such good hap! Nay, only Tabby came down to see the master, and brought her claws with her."

"Scrat him well, I hope?"

"Whipped him, and laid on pretty hard to boot."

"Why, you never mean it, real true, be sure!"

"Be sure I do. He's a-bed this morrow."

"I have my doubts if there'll be many tears shed in Staplehurst," said Mistress Final, laughing, as she went past with a plate of biscuit-bread, which, to judge from the receipt for making it, must have been very like our sponge cake.

"He's none so much loved of his neighbours," remarked Nicholas White, who kept a small ironmonger's shop, to which he added the sale of such articles as wood, wicker-work, crockery, and musical instruments.

The shorter and livelier of the travellers spoke for the first time.

"Pray you, who is this greatly beloved master?"

John Fishcock, the butcher, replied. "His name is Benden, and the folks be but ill-affected to him for his hard ways and sorry conditions."

"Hard!—in what manner, trow?"

"Nay, you'd best ask my neighbour here, whose landlord he is."

"And who'd love a sight better to deal with his mistress than himself," said Collet, answering the appeal. "I say not he's unjust, look you, but he's main hard, be sure. A farthing under the money, or a day over the time, and he's no mercy."

"Ah, the mistress was good to poor folks, bless her!" said Banks.

"She's dead, is she?" asked the stranger.

"No, she's away," replied Banks shortly.

"Back soon?" suggested the stranger.

John Banks had moved away. There was a peculiar gleam in his questioner's eye which he did not admire. But Collet, always unsuspicious, and not always discreet, replied without any idea of reserve.

"You'd best ask Dick o' Dover that, for none else can tell you."

"Ah, forsooth!" replied the stranger, apparently more interested than ever. "I heard as we came there were divers new doctrine folks at Staplehurst. She is one of them, belike?—and the master holds with the old? 'Tis sore pity folks should not agree to differ, and hold their several opinions in peace."

"Ah, it is so," said unsuspicious Collet.

"Pray you, who be the chief here of them of the new learning? We be strangers in these parts, and should be well a-paid to know whither we may seek our friends. Our hostess here, I am aware, is of them; but for others I scarce know. The name of White was dropped in mine hearing, and likewise Fishcock; who be they, trow? And dwells there not a certain Mistress Brandridge, or some such?—and a Master Hall or Ball—some whither in this neighbourhood, that be friends unto such as love not the papistical ways?"

"Look you now, I'll do you to wit all thereanent," said Collet confidentially. "For Fishcock, that was he that first spake unto you; he is a butcher, and dwelleth nigh the church. Nicholas White, yon big man yonder, that toppeth most of his neighbours, hath an ironmongery shop a-down in the further end of the village. Brandridge have we not: but Mistress Bradbridge—"

"Mistress, here's your master a-wanting you!" came suddenly in John Banks' clear tones; and Collette, hastily lifting her basket, and apologising for the sudden termination of her usefulness, departed quickly.

"She that hath hastened away is Mistress Wilson, methinks?" asked the inquisitive traveller of the person next him, who happened to be Mary Banks.

Mary looked quietly up into the animated face, and glanced at his companion also before replying. Then she said quietly—

"No, my master; Mistress Wilson is not now here."

"Then what name hath she?"

"I cry you mercy, Master; I have no time to tarry."

The grave man in the corner gave a grim smile as Mary turned away.

"You took not much by that motion, Malledge," he said in a low tone.

"I took a good deal by the former," replied Malledge, with a laugh. "Beside, I lacked it not; I wis well the name of my useful friend that is now gone her way. I did but ask to draw on more talk. But one matter I have not yet."

These words were spoken in an undertone, audible only to the person to whom they were addressed; and the speaker turned back to join in the general conversation. But before they had obtained any further information, the well-known sounds of the hunt came through the open door, and the whole company turned forth to see the hunters and hounds go by. Most of them did not return, but dispersed in the direction of their various homes, and from the few who did nothing was to be drawn.

John Banks walked away with Nicholas White. "Saw you those twain?" he asked, when they had left the White Hart a little way behind them. "The strange men? Ay, I saw them."

"I misdoubt if they come for any good purpose."

"Ay so?" said Nicholas in apparent surprise. "What leads you to that thought, trow?"

"I loved not neither of their faces; nor I liked not of their talk. That shorter man was for ever putting questions anent the folks in this vicinage that loved the Gospel; and Collet Pardue told him more than she should, or I mistake."

Nicholas White smiled. "I reckoned you were in some haste to let her wit that her master wanted her," he said.

"I was that. I was in a hurry to stop her tongue."

"Well!" said the ironmonger after a short pause, "the Lord keep His own!"

"Amen!" returned the mason. "But methinks, friend, the Lord works not many miracles to save even His own from traps whereinto they have run with their eyes open."

They walked on for a few minutes in silence. "What think you," asked White, "is come of Mistress Benden?"

"Would I wist!" answered Banks. "Master Hall saith he'll never let be till he find her, without he be arrest himself."

"That will he, if he have not a care."

"I'm not so sure," said Banks, "that those two in the White Hart could not have told us an' they would."

"Good lack!—what count you then they be?"

"I reckon that they be of my Lord Cardinal's men."

"Have you any ground for that fantasy?"

"Methought I saw the nether end of a mitre, broidered on the sleeve of the shorter man, where his cloak was caught aside upon the settle knob. Look you, I am not sure; but I'm 'feared lest it so be."

"Jack, couldst thou stand the fire?"

"I wis not, Nichol. Could you?"

"I cast no doubt I could do all things through Christ, nor yet that without Christ I could do nothing."

"It may come close, ere long," said Banks gravely.

The two travellers, meanwhile, had mounted their horses, and were riding in the direction of Goudhurst. A third man followed them, leading a baggage-horse. As they went slowly along, the taller man said—

"Have you all you need, now, Malledge?"

"All but one matter, Master Sumner—we know not yet where Hall dwelleth. Trust me, but I coveted your grave face, when we heard tell of Tabby horsewhipping yon Benden!"

"He hath his demerits," said the sumner,—that is, the official who served the summonses to the ecclesiastical courts.

"Of that I cast no doubt; nor care I if Tabby thrash him every day, for my part. When come we in our proper persons, to do our work?"

"That cannot I tell. We must first make report to my Lord of Dover."

A young girl and a little child came tripping down the road. The short man drew bridle and addressed them.

"Pray you, my pretty maids, can you tell me where dwelleth Mistress Bradbridge? I owe her a trifle of money, and would fain pay the same."

"Oh yes, sir!" said little Patience Bradbridge eagerly; "she's my mother. She dwells in yon white house over the field yonder."

"And Master Roger Hall, where dwelleth he?"

Penuel Pardue hastily stopped her little friend's reply.

"Master Hall is not now at home, my masters, so it should be to no purpose you visit his house. I give you good-morrow."

"Wise maid!" said Malledge with a laugh, when the girls were out of hearing. "If all were as close as thou, we should thrive little."

"They are all in a story!" said the sumner.

"Nay, not all," replied Malledge. "We have one to thank. But truly, they are a close-mouthed set, the most of them."

Chapter Seventeen.

The Justice is indiscreet.

"Methinks we be like to have further troubles touching religion in these parts. Marry, I do marvel what folks would be at, that they cannot be content to do their duty, and pay their dues, and leave the cure of their souls to the priest. As good keep a dog and bark thyself, say I, as pay dues to the priest and take thought for thine own soul."

The speaker was Mr Justice Roberts, and he sat at supper in his brother's house, one of a small family party, which consisted, beside the brothers, of their sister, Mistress Collenwood, Mistress Grena Holland, Gertrude, and Pandora. The speech was characteristic of the speaker. The Justice was by no means a bad man, as men go—and all of them do not go very straight in the right direction—but he made one mistake which many are making in our own day; he valued peace more highly than truth. His decalogue was a monologue, consisting but of one commandment: Do your duty. What a man's duty was, the Justice did not pause to define. Had he been required to do so, his dissection of that difficult subject would probably have run in three grooves—go to church; give alms; keep out of quarrels.

"It were verily good world, Master Justice, wherein every man should do his duty," was the answer of Mistress Grena, delivered in that slightly prim and didactic fashion which was characteristic of her.

"What is duty?" concisely asked Mistress Collenwood, who was by some ten years the elder of her brothers, and therefore the eldest of the company.

Gertrude's eyes were dancing with amusement; Pandora only looked interested.

"Duty," said Mr Roberts, the host, "is that which is due."

"To whom?" inquired his sister.

"To them unto whom he oweth it," was the reply; "first, to God; after Him, to all men."

"Which of us doth that?" said Mistress Collenwood softly, looking round the table.

Mistress Grena shook her head in a way which said, "Very few—not I."

Had Gertrude lived three hundred years later, she would have said what now she only thought—"I am sure *I* do my duty." But in 1557 young ladies were required to "hear, see, and say nought," and for one of them to join unasked in the conversation of her elders would have been held to be shockingly indecorous. The rule for girls' behaviour was too strict in that day; but if a little of it could be infused into the very lax code of the present time, when little misses offer their opinions on subjects of which they know nothing, and unblushingly differ from, or even contradict their mothers, too often without rebuke, it would be a decided improvement on social manners.

"Which of the folks in these parts be not doing their duty?" asked Mr Roberts of his brother.

"You know Benden of Briton's Mead?" replied the Justice.

"By sight; I am not well acquaint with him."

"Is he not an hard man, scarce well liked?" said his sister.

"True enough, as you shall say ere my tale come to an end. This Benden hath a wife—a decent Woman enough, as all men do confess, save that she is bitten somewhat by certain heretical notions that the priest cannot win her to lay by; will not come to mass, and so forth; but in all other fashions of good repute: and what doth this brute her husband but go himself to the Bishop, and beg—I do ensure you, beg his Lordship that this his wife may be arrest and lodged in prison. And in prison she is, and hath so been now these three or four months, on the sworn information of her own husband. 'Tis monstrous!"

"Truly, most shocking!" said Mistress Grena, cutting up the round of beef. The lady of the house always did the carving.

"Ah! As saith the old proverb: 'There is no worse pestilence than a familiar enemy,'" quoted the host.

"Well!" continued the Justice, with an amused look: "but now cometh a good jest, whereof I heard but yester-even. This Mistress Benden hath two brothers, named Hall—Roger and Thomas—one of whom dwelleth at Frittenden, and the other at yon corner house in Staplehurst, nigh to the Second Acre Close. Why, to be sure, he is your manager—that had I forgot."

Mr Roberts nodded. Pandora had pricked up her ears at the name of Hall, and now began to listen intently. Mistress Benden, of whom she heard for the first time, must be an aunt of her *protégée,* little Christabel.

"This Thomas Hall hath a wife, by name Tabitha, that the lads hereabout call Tabby, and by all accounts a right cat with claws is she. She, I hear, went up to Briton's Mead a two-three days gone, or maybe something more, and gave good Master Benden a taste of her horsewhip, that he hath since kept his bed—rather, I take it, from sulkiness than soreness, yet I dare be bound she handled him neatly. Tabitha is a woman of strong build, and lithe belike, that I would as lief not be horsewhipped by. Howbeit, what shall come thereof know I not. Very like she thought it should serve to move him to set Mistress Alice free: but she may find, and he belike, that 'tis easier to set a stone a-rolling down the hill than to stay it. The matter is now in my Lord of Dover's hands; and without Mistress Tabitha try her whip on him—"

Both gentlemen laughed. Pandora was deeply interested, as she recalled little Christie's delicate words, that Aunt Alice was "away at present." The child evidently would not say more. Pandora made up her mind that she would go and see Christie again as soon as possible, and meanwhile she listened for any information that she might give her.

"What is like to come of the woman, then?" said Mr Roberts, "apart from Mistress Tabitha and her whip?"

"Scarce release, I count," said the Justice gravely. "She hath been moved from the gaol; and that doubtless meaneth, had into straiter keeping."

"Poor fools!" said his brother, rather pityingly than scornfully.

"Ay, 'tis strange, in very deed, they cannot let be this foolish meddling with matters too high for them. If the woman would but conform and go to church, I hear, her womanish fantasies should very like be overlooked. Good lack I can a man not believe as he list, yet hold his tongue and be quiet, and not bring down the laws on his head?" concluded the Justice somewhat testily.

There was a pause, during which all were silent—from very various motives. Mr Roberts was thinking rather sadly that the only choice offered to men in those days was a choice of evils. He had never wished to conform—never would have done so, had he been let alone: but a man must look out for his safety, and take care of his property—of course he must!—and if the authorities made it impossible for him to do so with a good conscience, why, the fault was theirs, not his. Thus argued Mr Roberts, forgetting that the man makes a poor bargain who gains the whole world and loses himself. The Justice and Gertrude were simply enjoying their supper. No scruples of any kind disturbed their slumbering consciences. Mistress Collenwood's face gave no indication of her thoughts. Pandora was reflecting chiefly upon Christabel.

But there was one present whose conscience had been asleep, and was just waking to painful life. For nearly four years had Grena Holland soothed her many misgivings by some such reasoning as that of Mr Justice Roberts. She had conformed outwardly: had not merely abstained from contradictory speeches, but had gone to mass, had attended the confessional, had bowed down before images of wood and stone, and all the time had comforted herself by imagining that God saw her heart, and knew that she did not really believe in any of these things, but only acted thus for safety's sake. Now, all at once, she knew not how, it came on her as by a flash of lightning that she was on the road that leadeth to destruction, and not content with that, was bearing her young nieces along with her. She loved those girls as if she had been their own mother. Grave, self-contained, and undemonstrative as she was, she would almost have given her life for either, but especially for Pandora, who in face, and to some extent in character, resembled her dead mother, the sister who had been the darling of Grena Holland's heart. She recalled with keen pain the half-astonished, half-shrinking look on Pandora's face, as she had followed her to mass on the first holy-day after her return from Lancashire. Grena knew well that at Shardeford Hall, her mother's house in Lancashire, Pandora would never have been required to attend mass, but would have been taught that it was "a fond fable and a dangerous deceit." And now, she considered, that look had passed from the girl's face; she went silently, not eagerly on the one hand, yet unprotestingly, even by look, on the other. Forward into the possible future went Grena's imagination—to the prison, and the torture-chamber, and the public disgrace, and the awful death of fire. How could she bear those, either for herself or for Pandora?

These painful meditations were broken in upon by a remark from the Justice.

"There is some strong ale brewing, I warrant you, for some of our great doctors and teachers of this vicinage. I heard t'other day, from one that shall be nameless—indeed, I would not mention the matter, but we be all friends and good Catholics here—"

Mistress Collenwood's eyes were lifted a moment from her plate, but then went down again in silence.

"Well, I heard say two men of my Lord Cardinal's had already been a-spying about these parts, for to win the names of such as were suspect: and divers in and nigh Staplehurst shall hear more than they wot of, ere many days be over. Mine hostess at the White Hart had best look out, and—well, there be others; more in especial this Master Ro— Come, I'll let be the rest."

"I trust you have not said too much already," remarked Mr Roberts rather uneasily.

That the Justice also feared he had been indiscreet was shown by his slight testiness in reply.

"Tush! how could I? There's never a serving-man in the chamber, and we be all safe enough. Not the tail of a word shall creep forth, be sure."

"'Three may keep counsel, if twain be away,'" said Mr Roberts, shaking his head with a good-humoured smile.

"They do not alway then," added Mistress Collenwood drily.

"Well, well!" said the Justice, "you wot well enough, every one of you, the matter must go no further. Mind you, niece Gertrude, you slip it not forth to some chattering maid of your acquaintance."

"Oh, I am safe enough, good Uncle," laughed Gertrude.

"Indeed, I hope we be all discreet in such dangerous matters," added Mistress Grena.

Only Mrs Collenwood and Pandora were silent.

Chapter Eighteen.

Out of heart.

"Aunt Grena," said Pandora Roberts, "if it stand with your pleasure, may I have leave to visit little Christabel Hall this fine morrow?"

"Thou shouldst, my dear heart, with my very good will," was the kindly answer; "but misfortunately, at this time I am not in case to accompany thee."

Pandora did not reply, but she looked greatly disappointed, when her aunt, Mistress Collenwood, suggested—

"Could not old Osmund go with her, Grena?"

"He might, if it were matter of grave concern," replied Mistress Grena, in a tone which indicated that the concern would have to be very grave indeed.

"Well, Dorrie, thou mayest clear those troubled eyes," said Mistress Collenwood with a smile: "for I myself will accompany thee to visit thy friend."

"You, Aunt Francis? Oh, I thank you!" said Pandora joyfully, passing in a moment from distress to delight.

In half-an-hour the horses were at the door. Not much was said during the ride to Staplehurst, except that Pandora told her aunt that Christabel was an invalid child, and that her father was the manager at the cloth-works. Christie, who of course was always at home, was rejoiced to see her friend; and Mistress Collenwood inquired closely into her ailments, ending with the suggestion, which she desired might be conveyed to her father, that Christie should rub her limbs with oil of swallows, and take a medicine compounded of plantain water and "powder of swine's claws."

"Father's in the house," said Christie. "He had to return back for some papers the master desired."

Roger Hall confirmed her words by coming into the room in a few minutes, with the papers in his hand which he had been sent to seek. He made a reverence to his master's relatives.

"Master Hall," said Mrs Collenwood, "I would gladly have a word with you touching your little maid's ailments."

Roger detected her desire to say something to him out of Christie's hearing, and led her to the kitchen, which was just then empty, as Nell was busy in the wash-house outside.

"I pray you to bar the door," said Mrs Collenwood.

Roger obeyed, rather wondering at the request. Mrs Collenwood shortly told him that she thought the oil of swallows might strengthen Christie's limbs, and the medicine improve her general health, but she so quickly dismissed that subject that it was plain she had come for something else. Roger waited respectfully till she spoke.

Speech seemed to be difficult to the lady. Twice she looked up and appeared to be on the point of speaking; and twice her eyes dropped, her face flushed, but her voice remained silent. At last she said—

"Master Hall, suffer me to ask if you have friends in any other county?"

Roger was considerably surprised at the question.

"I have, my mistress," said he, "a married sister that dwelleth in Norfolk, but I have not seen her these many years."

He thought she must mean that Christie's health would be better in some other climate, which was a strange idea to him, at a time when change of air was considered almost dangerous.

"Norfolk—should scarce serve," said the lady, in a timid, hesitating manner. "The air of the Green Yard at Norwich (where stood the Bishop's prison for heretics) is not o'er good. I think not of your little maid's health, Master Hall, but of your own."

Roger Hall was on the point of asserting with some perplexity and much amazement, that his health was perfect, and he required neither change nor medicine, when the real object of these faltering words suddenly flashed on him. His heart seemed to leap into his mouth, then to retreat to its place, beating fast.

"My mistress," he said earnestly, "I took not at the first your kindly meaning rightly, but I count I so do now. If so be, I thank you more than words may tell. But I must abide at my post. My sister Alice is not yet found; and should I be taken from the child"—his voice trembled for a moment—"God must have care of her."

"I will have a care of her, in that case," said Mrs Collenwood. "Master Hall, we may speak freely. What you are, I am. Now I have put my life in your hands, and I trust you to be true."

"I will guard it as mine own," answered Roger warmly, "and I give you the most heartiest thanks, my mistress, that a man wot how to utter. But if I may ask you, be any more in danger? My brother, and Master White, and Mistress Final—"

"All be in danger," was the startling answer, "that hold with us. But the one only name that I have heard beside yours, is mine hostess of the White Hart."

"Mistress Final? I reckoned so much. I will have a word with her, if it may be, on my way back to Cranbrook, and bid her send word to the others. Alack the day! how long is Satan to reign, and wrong to triumph?"

"So long as God will," replied Mrs Collenwood. "So long as His Church hath need of the cleansing physic shall it be ministered to her. When she is made clean, and white, and tried, then—no longer.

God grant, friend, that you and I may not fail Him when the summons cometh for us—'The Master calleth for thee.'"

"Amen!" said Roger Hall.

In the parlour Pandora said to Christabel—

"Dear child, thou mayest speak freely to me of thine Aunt Alice. I know all touching her."

"O Mistress Pandora! wot you where she is?"

Pandora was grieved to find from Christie's eager exclamation that she had, however innocently, roused the child's hopes only to be disappointed.

"No, my dear heart," she said tenderly, "not that, truly. I did but signify that I knew the manner of her entreatment, and where she hath been lodged."

"Father can't find her anywhere," said Christie sorrowfully. "He went about two whole days, but he could hear nothing of her at all."

"Our Father in Heaven knows where she is, my child. He shall not lose sight of her, be well assured."

"But she can't see Him!" urged Christie tearfully.

"Truth, sweeting. Therefore rather 'blessed are they that have not seen, and yet have believed.' Consider how hard the blessed Paul was tried, and how hard he must have found faith, and yet how fully he did rely on our Saviour Christ."

"I don't think Saint Paul was ever tried this way," said Christie in her simplicity. "And his sister's son knew where he was, and could get at him. They weren't as ill off as me and Father."

"Poor old Jacob did not know where Joseph was," suggested Pandora.

"Well, ay," admitted Christie. "But Jacob was an old man; he wasn't a little maid. And Joseph came all right, after all. Beside, he was a lad, and could stand things. Aunt Alice isn't strong. And she hasn't been nobody's white child (favourite) as Joseph was; I am sure Uncle Edward never made her a coat of many colours. Mistress Pandora, is it very wicked of me to feel as if I could not bear to look at Uncle Edward, and hope that he will never, never, never come to see us any more?"

"'Tis not wicked to hate a man's sinful deeds, dear heart; but we have need to beware that we hate not the sinner himself."

"I can't tell how to manage that," said Christie. "I can't put Uncle Edward into one end of my mind, and the ill way he hath used dear Aunt Alice into the other. He's a bad, wicked man, or he never could have done as he has."

"Suppose he be the very worst man that ever lived, Christie—and I misdoubt if he be so—but supposing it, wouldst thou not yet wish that God should forgive him?"

"Well; ay, I suppose I would," said Christie, in a rather uncertain tone; "but if Uncle Edward's going to Heaven, I do hope the angels will keep him a good way off Aunt Alice, and Father, and me. I don't think it would be so pleasant if he were there."

Pandora smiled.

"We will leave that, sweet heart, till thou be there," she said.

And just as she spoke Mrs Collenwood returned to the parlour. She chatted pleasantly for a little while with Christie, and bade her not lose heart concerning her Aunt Alice.

"The Lord will do His best for His own, my child," she said, as they took leave of Christabel; "but after all, mind thou, His best is not always our best. Nay; at times it is that which seems to us the worst. Yet I cast no doubt we shall bless Him for it, and justify all His ways, when we stand on the mount of God, and look back along the road that we have traversed. 'All the paths of the Lord are mercy and truth unto such as keep His covenant and his testimonies.'"

Some such comfort as those words of God can give was sorely needed by Roger Hall. To use a graphic expression of his day, he was "well-nigh beat out of heart." He had visited all the villages within some distance, and had tramped to and fro in Canterbury, and could hear nothing. He had not as yet hinted to any one his own terrible apprehension that Alice might have been removed to London for trial. If so, she would come into the brutal and relentless hands of Bishop Bonner, and little enough hope was there in that case. The only chance, humanly speaking, then lay in the occasional visits paid by Cardinal Pole to Smithfield, for the purpose of rescuing, from Bonner's noble army of martyrs, the doomed who belonged to his own diocese. And that was a poor hope indeed.

There were two important holy-days left in February, and both these Roger spent in Canterbury, despite the warning of his impending arrest if he ventured in that direction. On the latter of these two he paid special attention to the cathedral precincts. It was possible that Alice might be imprisoned in the house of one of the canons or prebendaries; and if so, there was a faint possibility that she might be better treated than in the gaol. Everywhere he listened for her voice. At every window he gazed earnestly, in the hope of seeing her face. He saw and heard nothing.

As he turned away to go home, on the evening of Saint Matthias', it struck him that perhaps, if he were to come very early in the morning, the town would be more silent, and there might be a better likelihood of detecting the sound of one voice among many. But suppose she were kept in solitary confinement—how then could he hope to hear it?

Very, very down-hearted was Roger as he rode home. He met two or three friends, who asked, sympathetically, “No news yet, Master Hall?” and he felt unable to respond except by a mournful shake of the head.

“Well, be sure! what can have come of the poor soul?” added Emmet Wilson. And Roger could give no answer.

What could have become of Alice Benden?

Chapter Nineteen.

Eureka!

In the court where the prebendaries' chambers were situated, within the Cathedral Close at Canterbury, was an underground vault, known as Monday's Hole. Here the stocks were kept, but the place was very rarely used as a prison. A paling, four feet and a half in height, and three feet from the window, cut off all glimpses of the outer world from any person within. A little short straw was strewn on the floor, between the stocks and the wall, which formed the only bed of any one there imprisoned. It was a place where a man of any humanity would scarcely have left his dog; cold, damp, dreary, depressing beyond measure.

That litter of straw, on the damp stones, had been for five weary weeks the bed of Alice Benden. She was allowed no change of clothes, and all the pittance given her for food was a halfpenny worth of bread, and a farthing's worth of drink. At her own request she had been permitted to receive her whole allowance in bread; and water, not over clean nor fresh, was supplied for drinking. No living creature came near her save her keeper, who was the bell-ringer at the cathedral—if we except the vermin which held high carnival in the vault, and were there in extensive numbers. It was a dreadful place for any human being to live in; how dreadful for an educated and delicate gentlewoman, accustomed to the comforts of civilisation, it is not easy to imagine.

But to the coarser tortures of physical deprivation and suffering had been added the more refined torments of heart and soul. During four of those five weeks all God's waves and billows had gone over Alice Benden. She felt herself forsaken of God and man alike—out of mind, like the slain that lie in the grave—forgotten even by the Lord her Shepherd.

One visitor she had during that time, who had by no means forgotten her. Satan has an excellent memory, and never lacks leisure to tempt God's children. He paid poor Alice a great deal of attention. How, he asked her, was it possible that a just God, not to say a merciful Saviour, could have allowed her to come into such misery? Had the Lord's hand waxed short? Here were the persecutors, many of them ungodly men, robed in soft silken raiment, and faring sumptuously every day; their beds were made of the finest down, they had all that heart could wish; while she lay upon dirty straw in this damp hole, not a creature knowing what had become of her. Was this all she had received as the reward of serving God? Had she not tried to do His will, and to walk before Him with a perfect heart? and this was what she got for it, from Him who could have swept away her persecutors by a word, and lifted her by another to the height of luxury and happiness.

Poor Alice was overwhelmed. Her bodily weakness—of which Satan may always be trusted to take advantage—made her less fit to cope with him, and for a time she did not guess who it was that suggested all these wrong and miserable thoughts. She "grievously bewailed" herself, and, as people often do, nursed her distress as if it were something very dear and precious.

But God had not forgotten Alice Benden. She was not going to be lost—she, for whom Christ died. She was only to be purified, and made white, and tried. He led her to find comfort in His own Word, the richest of earthly comforters. One night Alice began to repeat to herself the forty-second Psalm. It seemed just made for her. It was the cry of a sore heart, shut in by enemies, and shut out from hope and pleasure. Was not that just her case?

"Why art thou so full of heaviness, O my soul? and why art thou so disquieted within me? Put thy trust in God!"

A little relieved, she turned next to the seventy-seventh Psalm. She had no Bible; nothing but what her well-stored memory gave her. Ah! what would have become of Alice Benden in those dark hours, had her memory been filled with all kinds of folly, and not with the pure, unerring Word of God? This Psalm exactly suited her.

"Will the Lord absent Himself for ever?—and will He be no more entreated? Is His mercy clean gone for ever?—and is His promise come utterly to an end for evermore? Hath God forgotten to be gracious?—and will He shut up His loving-kindness in displeasure? And I said, It is mine infirmity: but I will remember the years of the right hand of the Most Highest."

A light suddenly flashed, clear and warm, into the weak, low, dark heart of poor lonely Alice. "It is mine infirmity!" Not God's infirmity—not God's forgetfulness! "No, Alice, never that," it seemed just as if somebody said to her: "it is only your poor blind heart here in the dark, that cannot see the joy and deliverance that are coming to you—that must come to all God's people: but He who dwells in the immortal light, and beholds the end from the beginning, knows how to come and set you free—knows when to come and save you."

The tune changed now. Satan was driven away. The enemy whom Alice Benden had seen that day, and from whom she had suffered so sorely, she should see again no more for ever. From that hour all was joy and hope.

"I will magnify Thee, O God my King, and praise Thy name for ever and ever!"

That was the song she sang through her prison bars in the early morning of the 25th of February. The voice of joy and thanksgiving reached where the moan of pain had not been able to penetrate, to an intently listening ear a few yards from the prison. Then an answering voice of delight came to her from without.

"Alice! Alice! I have found thee!"

Alice looked up, to see her brother Roger's head and shoulders above the paling which hid all but a strip of sky from her gaze.

"Hast thou been a-searching for me all these weeks, Roger?"

"That have I, my dear heart, ever since thou wast taken from the gaol. How may I win at thee?"

"That thou canst not, Hodge. But we may talk a moment, for my keeper, that is the bell-ringer of the minster, is now at his work there, and will not return for an half-hour well reckoned. Thou wert best come at those times only, or I fear thou shalt be taken."

"I shall not be taken till God willeth," said Roger. "I will come again to thee in a moment."

He ran quickly out of the precincts, and into the first baker's shop he saw, where he bought a small loaf of bread. Into it he pushed five fourpenny pieces, then called groats, and very commonly current. Then he fixed the loaf on the end of his staff, and so passed it through the bars to Alice. This was all he could do.

"My poor dear heart, hast thou had no company in all this time?"

"I have had Satan's company a weary while," she answered, "but this last night he fled away, and the Lord alone is with me."

"God be praised!" said Roger. "And how farest thou?"

"Very ill touching the body; very well touching the soul."

"What matter can I bring thee to thy comfort?"

"What I lack most is warmth and cleanly covering. I have no chance even to wash me, and no clothes to shift me. But thou canst bring me nought, Hodge, I thank thee, and I beseech thee, essay it not. How fares little Christie?—and be all friends well?"

"All be well, I thank the Lord, and Christie as her wont is. It shall do her a power of good to hear thou art found. Dost know when thou shalt appear before the Bishop?"

"That do I not, Hodge. It will be when God willeth, and to the end He willeth; and all that He willeth is good. I have but to endure to the end: He shall see to all the rest. Farewell, dear brother; it were best that thou shouldst not tarry."

As Roger came within sight of Staplehurst on his return, he saw a woman walking rapidly along the road to meet him, and when he came a little nearer, he perceived that it was Tabitha. Gently urging his horse forward, they met in a few minutes. The expression of Tabitha's face alarmed Roger greatly. She was not wont to look so moved and troubled. Grim and sarcastic, even angry, he had seen her many times; but grieved and sorrowful—this was not like Tabitha. Roger's first fear was that she had come to give him some terrible news of Christie. Yet her opening words were not those of pain or terror.

"The Lord be thanked you were not here this day, Roger Hall!" was Tabitha's strange greeting.

"What hath happed?" demanded Roger, stopping his horse.

"What hath happed is that Staplehurst is swept nigh clean of decent folks. Sheriffs been here—leastwise his man, Jeremy Green—and took off a good dozen of Gospellers."

"Tom—Christie?" fell tremulously from Roger's lips.

"Neither of them. I looked to *them,* and old Jeremy knows me. I heard tell of their coming, and I had matters in readiness to receive them. I reckon Jerry had an inkling of that red-hot poker and the copper of boiling water I'd prepared for his comfort; any way, he passed our house by, and at yours he did but ask if you were at home, and backed out, as pleasant as you please, when Nell made answer 'Nay.'"

"Then whom have they taken?"

"Mine hostess of the White Hart gat the first served. Then they went after Nichol White, and Nichol Pardue."

"Pardue!" exclaimed Roger.

"Ay, Nichol: did not touch Collet. But they took Emmet Wilson, and Fishwick, butcher, and poor Sens Bradbridge, of all simple folks."

"And what became of her poor little maids?" asked Roger pityingly.

"Oh, Collet's got them. I'd have fetched 'em myself if she hadn't. They've not taken Jack Banks, nor Mall. Left 'em for next time, maybe."

"Well, I am thankful they took not you, Tabitha."

"Me? They'd have had to swallow my red-hot poker afore they took me. I count they frighted Christie a bit, fearing they'd have you; but I went to see after the child, and peaced her metely well ere I came thence."

"I am right thankful to you, sister. Tabitha, I have found Alice."

"You have so?—and where is she?"

Roger gave a detailed account of the circumstances.

"Seems to me they want a taste of the poker there," said Tabitha in her usual manner. "I'll buy a new one, so that I run not out of stock ere customers come. But I scarce think old Jeremy'll dare come a-nigh me; it'll be Sheriff himself, I reckon, when that piece of work's to be done. If they come to your house, just you bid Nell set the poker in the fire, and run over for me, and you keep 'em in talk while I come. Or a good kettle of boiling water 'd do as well—I'm no wise nice which it is—or if she'd a kettle of hot pitch handy, that's as good as anything."

"I thank you for your counsel, Tabitha. I trust there may be no need."

"And I the like: but you might as well have the pitch ready."

Chapter Twenty.

Unstable as water.

"And I hope, my dear son," said the Rev. Mr Bastian, with a face and voice as mellifluous as a honeycomb, "that all the members of your household are faithful, and well affected towards the Church our mother?"

The Rev. Mr Bastian chose his words well. If he had said, "as faithful as yourself," Mr Roberts might have assented, with an interior conviction that his own faithfulness was not without its limits. He left no such loophole of escape. Mr Roberts could only reply that he entertained a similar hope. But whatever his hopes might be, his expectations on that score were not extensive. Mr Roberts had the nature of the ostrich, and imagined that if he shut his eyes to the thing he wished to avoid seeing, he thereby annihilated its existence. Deep down in his heart he held considerable doubts as concerned more than one member of his family; but the doubts were uncomfortable: so he put them to bed, drew the curtains, and told them to be good doubts and go to sleep. When children are treated in this manner, mothers and nurses know that sometimes they go to sleep. But sometimes they don't. And doubts are very much like children in that respect. Occasionally they consent to be smothered up and shelved aside; at other times they break out and become provokingly noisy. A good deal depends on the vitality of both the doubts and the children.

Mr Roberts's doubts and fears—for they went together—that all his household were not in a conformable state of mind, had hitherto gone to sleep at his bidding; but lately they had been more difficult to manage. He was uneasy about his sister, Mrs Collenwood; and with no diminution of his affection for her, was beginning to realise that his mind would be relieved when she ended her visit and went home. He feared her influence over Pandora. For Gertrude he had no fears. He knew, and so did the priest, that Gertrude was not the sort of girl to indulge in abstract speculations, religious or otherwise. So long as her new gown was not made in last year's fashion, and her mantua-maker did not put her off with Venice ribbon when she wanted Tours, it mattered nothing at all to Gertrude whether she attended mass or went to the nearest conventicle. Nor had the fears spread yet towards Mistress Grena, who still appeared at mass on Sunday and holy-days, though with many inward misgivings which she never spoke.

Perhaps the priest had sharper eyes than the easy-tempered master of Primrose Croft. But his tongue had lost nothing of its softness when he next inquired—

"And how long, my son, does your sister, Mistress Collenwood, abide with you?"

"Not much longer now, Father," replied the unhappy Mr Roberts, with a private resolution that his answer should be true if he could make it so.

Mr Bastian left that unpleasant topic, and proceeded to carry his queries into the servants' department, Mr Roberts growing more relieved as he proceeded. He had never observed any want of conformity among his servants, he assured the priest; so far as he knew, all were loyal to the Catholic Church. By that term both gentlemen meant, not the universal body of Christian believers (the real signification of the word), but that minority which blindly obeys the Pope, and being a minority, is of course not Catholic nor universal. When Mr Roberts's apprehensions had thus been entirely lulled to rest, the wily priest suddenly returned to the charge.

"I need not, I am fully ensured," he said in his suave manner, "ask any questions touching your daughters."

"Of that, Father," answered Mr Roberts quickly, "you must be a better judge than I. But I do most unfeignedly trust that neither of my maids hath given you any trouble by neglect of her religious duties? Gertrude, indeed, is so—"

"Mistress Gertrude hath not given me trouble," replied the priest. "Her worst failing is one common to maidens—a certain lack of soberness. But I cannot conceal from you, my son, that I am under some uneasiness of mind as touching her sister."

Mr Bastian's uneasiness was nothing to that of the man he was engaged in tormenting. The terrified mouse does not struggle more eagerly to escape the claws of the cat, than the suffering father of Pandora to avoid implicating her in the eyes of his insinuating confessor.

"Forsooth, Father, you do indeed distress me," said he. "If Pandora have heard any foolish talk on matters of religion, I would gladly break her from communication with any such of her acquaintance as can have been thus ill-beseen. Truly, I know not of any, and methought my sister Grena kept the maids full diligently, that they should not fall into unseemly ways. I will speak, under your good leave, with both of them, and will warn Pandora that she company not with such as seem like to have any power over her for evil."

"Well said, my son!" responded the priest, with a slight twinkle in his eye. "Therein shall you do well; and in especial if you report to me the names of any that you shall suspect to have ill-affected the maiden. And now, methinks, I must be on my way home."

Mr Roberts devoutly thanked all the saints when he heard it. The priest took up his hat, brushed a stray thread from its edge, and said, as he laid his hand upon his silver-headed stick—said it as though the idea had just occurred to him—

"You spake of Mistress Holland. She, of course, is true to holy Church beyond all doubts?"

Mr Roberts went back to his previous condition of a frightened mouse.

"In good sooth, Father, I make no question thereof, nor never so did. She conformeth in all respects, no doth she?"

The cat smiled to itself at the poor mouse's writhings under its playful pats.

"She conformeth—ay: but I scarce need warn you, my son, that there be many who conform outwardly, where the heart is not accordant with the actions. I trust, in very deed, that it were an unjust matter so to speak of Mistress Holland."

Saying which, the cat withdrew its paw, and suffered the mouse to escape to its hole until another little excitement should be agreeable to it. In other words, the priest said good-bye, and left Mr Roberts in a state of mingled relief for the moment and apprehension for the future. For a few minutes that unhappy gentleman sat lost in meditation. Then rising with a muttered exclamation, wherein "meddlesome praters" were the only words distinguishable, he went to the foot of the stairs, and called up them, "Pandora!"

"There, now! You'll hear of something!" said Gertrude to her sister, as she stood trying on a new apron before the glass. "You'd best go down. When Father's charitably-minded he says either 'Pan' or 'Dorrie.' 'Pandora' signifies he's in a taking."

"I have done nought to vex him that I know of," replied Pandora, rising from her knees before a drawer wherein she was putting some lace tidily away.

"Well, get not me in hot water," responded Gertrude. "Look you, Pan, were this lace not better to run athwart toward the left hand?"

"I cannot wait to look, True; I must see what Father would have."

As Pandora hastened downstairs, her aunt, Mrs Collenwood, came out of her room and joined her.

"I hear my brother calling you," she said. "I would fain have a word with him, so I will go withal."

The ladies found Mr Roberts wandering to and fro in the dining-room, with the aspect of a very dissatisfied man. He turned at once to his daughter.

"Pandora, when were you at confession?"

Pandora's heart beat fast. "Not this week, Father."

"Nor this month, maybe?"

"I am somewhat unsure, Father."

"Went you to mass on Saint Chad's Day?"

"Yes, Father."

"And this Saint Perpetua?"

"No, Father; I had an aching of mine head, you mind."

"Thomas," interjected Mrs Collenwood, before the examination could proceed further, "give me leave, pray you, to speak a word, which I desire to say quickly, and you can resume your questioning of Pandora at after. I think to return home Thursday shall be a se'nnight; and, your leave granted, I would fain carry Pan with me. Methinks this air is not entirely wholesome for her at this time; and unless I err greatly, it should maybe save her some troublement if she tarried with me a season. I pray you, consider of the same, and let me know your mind thereon as early as may stand with your conveniency: and reckon me not tedious if I urge you yet again not to debar the same without right good reason. I fear somewhat for the child, without she can change the air, and that right soon."

Pandora listened in astonishment. She was quite unconscious of bodily ailment, either present or likely to come. What could Aunt Frances mean? But Mr Roberts saw, what Pandora did not, a very significant look in his sister's eyes, which said, more plainly than her words, that danger of some kind lay in wait for her niece if she remained in Kent, and was to be expected soon. He fidgeted up and down the room for a moment, played nervously with an alms-dish on the side-board, took up Cicero's Orations and laid it down again, and at last said, in a tone which indicated relief from vexation—

"Well, well! Be it so, if you will. Make thee ready, then, child, to go with thine aunt. Doth Grena know your desire, Frank?"

"Grena and I have taken counsel," replied Mrs Collenwood, "and this is her avisement no less than mine."

"Settle it so, then. I thank you, Frank, for your care for the maid. When shall she return?"

"It were better to leave that for time to come. But, Thomas, I go about to ask a favour of you more."

"Go to! what is it?"

"That you will not name to any man Pandora's journey with me. Not to any man," repeated Mrs Collenwood, with a stress on the last two words.

Mr Roberts looked at her. Her eyes conveyed serious warning. He knew as well as if she had shouted the words in his ears that the real translation of her request was, "Do not tell the priest." But it was not safe to say it. Wherever there are Romish priests, there must be silent looks and tacit hints and unspoken understandings.

"Very good, Frances," he said: "I will give no man to wit thereof."

"I thank you right heartily, Tom. Should Dorrie abide here for your further satisfying, or may she go with me?"

"Go with you, go with you," answered Mr Roberts hastily, waving Pandora away. "No need any further—time presseth, and I have business to see to."

Mrs Collenwood smiled silently as she motioned to Pandora to pass out. Mr Roberts could scarcely have confessed more plainly that the priest had set him to a catechising of which he was but too thankful to be rid. “Poor Tom!” she said to herself.

Chapter Twenty One.

Check!

Pandora would have spoken as soon as they left the dining-room, but she was stopped by a motion of her aunt's hand. Mrs Collenwood took her into her own bedroom, shut and barred the door, glanced inside a hanging closet to see that no one was secreted there, and seating herself on the cushioned seat which ran round the inside of the bay window, signed to her niece to take a seat beside her.

"Now, Dorrie, speak thy desire."

"Aunt Frances, I am surprised with wonder! Pray you, what ail I, that I must quit home thus suddenly? I feel right well, and knew not there was aught ado with mine health."

Pandora's voice betrayed a little alarm. It certainly was a startling thing for a girl who felt and believed herself in excellent health, to hear suddenly that unless she had instant change of air, serious consequences might be expected to ensue.

Mrs Collenwood smiled—an affectionate, almost compassionate smile—as she patted Pandora's shoulder.

"Take thine heart to thee, Dorrie. Thou art not sick, and if I can have thee away in sufficient time, God allowing, thou shalt not be. But I fear, if thou tarry, thou mayest have an attack of a certain pestilence that is rife in Kent at this season."

"Pestilence, Aunt Frances! I never heard of no such going about. But if so, why I alone? There be Father, and True, and Aunt Grena—should they not go likewise?"

"No fear for Gertrude," answered Mrs Collenwood, almost sadly. "And not much, methinks, for thy father. I am lesser sure of thine

Aunt Grena: but I have not yet been able to prevail with her to accompany us."

"But what name hath this pestilence, under your good leave, Aunt Frances?"

"It is called, Dorrie—persecution."

The colour rose slowly in Pandora's cheeks, until her whole face was suffused.

"Methinks I take you now, Aunt," she said. "But, if I may have liberty to ask at you, wherefore think you Father and True to be safer than Aunt Grena and I?"

"Because they would yield, Dorrie. I misdoubt any charge brought against Gertrude; 'tis not such as she that come before religious tribunals. They will know they have her safe enough."

"Aunt Frances," said Pandora in a whisper, "think you I should not yield?"

"I hope thou wouldst not, Dorrie."

"But how wist you—how could you know," asked the girl passionately, "what I had kept so carefully concealed? How could you know that I hated to go to mass, and availed myself of every whit of excuse that should serve my turn to stay away from confession?—that I besought God every night, yea, with tears, to do away this terrible state of matters, and to grant us rulers under whom we might worship Him without fear, according to His will and word? I counted I had hidden mine heart from every eye but His. Aunt Frances, how *could* you know?"

Mrs Collenwood drew Pandora into her arms.

"Because, my child, I had done the same."

The girl's arms came round her aunt's neck, and their cheeks were pressed close.

"O Aunt Frances, I am so glad! I have so lacked one to speak withal herein! I have thought at times, if I had but one human creature to whom I might say a word!—and then there was nobody but God—I seemed driven to Him alone."

"That is blessed suffering, my dear heart, which drives souls to God; and there he will come with nought lesser. Dorrie, methinks thou scarce mindest thy mother?"

"Oh, but I do, Aunt! She was the best and dearest mother that ever was. True loves not to talk of her, nor of any that is dead; so that here also I had to shut up my thoughts within myself; but I mind her—ay, that I do!"

"Niece, when she lay of her last sickness, she called me to her, and quoth she—'Frances, I have been sore troubled for my little Dorrie: but methinks now I have let all go, and have left her in the hands of God. Only if ever the evil days should come again, and persecution arise because of the witness of Jesus, and the Word of God, and the testimony which we hold—tell her, if you find occasion, as her mother's last dying word to her, that she hold fast the word of the truth of the Gospel, and be not moved away therefrom, neither by persuading nor threatening. 'Tis he that overcometh, and he only, that shall have the crown of life.' Never till now, Pandora, my dear child, have I told thee these words of thy dead and saintly mother. I pray God lay them on thine heart, that thou mayest stand in the evil day—yea, whether thou escape these things or no, thou mayest stand before the Son of Man at His coming."

Pandora had hidden her face on Mrs Collenwood's shoulder.

"Oh, *do* pray, Aunt Frances!" she said, with a sob.

The days for a week after that were very busy ones. Every day some one or two bags were packed, and quietly conveyed at nightfall by

Mrs Collenwood's own man to an inn about four miles distant. Pandora was kept indoors, except one day, when she went with Mrs Collenwood to take leave of Christie. That morning the priest called and expressed a wish to speak to her: but being told that she was gone to see a friend, said he would call again the following day. Of this they were told on their return. Mrs Collenwood's cheeks paled a little; then, with set lips, and a firm step, she sought her brother in his closet, or as we should say, his study.

"Tom," she said, when the door was safely shut, "we must be gone this night."

Mr Roberts looked up in considerable astonishment.

"This night!—what mean you, Frances? The clouds be gathering for rain, and your departure was fixed for Thursday."

"Ay, the clouds be gathering," repeated Mrs Collenwood meaningly, "and I am 'feared Pandora, if not I, may be caught in the shower. Have you not heard that Father Bastian desired to speak with her whilst we were hence this morrow? We must be gone, Tom, ere he come again."

Mr Roberts, who was busy with his accounts, set down a five as the addition of eight and three, with a very faint notion of what he was doing.

"Well!" he said, in an undecided manner. "Well! it is—it is not—it shall look—"

"How should it look," replied Mrs Collenwood, with quiet incisiveness, "to see Pandora bound to the stake for burning?"

Mr Roberts threw out his hands as if to push away the terrible suggestion.

"It may come to that, Tom, if we tarry. For, without I mistake, the girl is not made of such willowy stuff as—some folks be."

She just checked herself from saying, "as you are."

Mr Roberts passed his fingers through his hair, in a style which said, as plainly as words, that he was about at his wits' end. Perhaps he had not far to go to reach that locality.

"Good lack!" he said. "Dear heart!—well-a-day!"

"She will be safe with me," said her aunt, "for a time at least. And if danger draw near there also, I can send her thence to certain friends of mine in a remote part amongst the mountains, where a priest scarce cometh once in three years. And ere that end, God may work changes in this world."

"Well, if it must be—"

"It must be, Tom; and it shall be for the best."

"It had been better I had wist nought thereof. They shall be sure to question me."

Mrs Collenwood looked with a smile of pitying contempt on the man who was weaker than herself. The contempt predominated at first: then it passed into pity.

"Thou shalt know nought more than now, Tom," she said quietly. "Go thou up, and get thee a-bed, but leave the key of the wicket-gate on this table."

"I would like to have heard you had gat safe away," said poor Mr Roberts, feeling in his pockets for the key.

"You would speedily hear if we did not," was the answer.

Mr Roberts sighed heavily as he laid down the key.

"Well, I did hope to keep me out of this mess. I had thought, by outward conforming, and divers rich gifts to the priest, and so forth— 'Tis hard a man cannot be at peace in his own house."

"'Tis far harder when he is not at peace in his own soul."

"Ah!" The tone of the exclamation said that was quite too good to expect, at any rate for the speaker.

Mrs Collenwood laid her hand on her brother's shoulder.

"Tom, we are parting for a long season—it may be for all time. Suffer me speak one word with thee, for the sake of our loving mother, and for her saintly sake that sleepeth in All Saints' churchyard, whose head lay on my bosom when her spirit passed to God. There will come a day, good brother, when thou shalt stand before an higher tribunal than that of my Lord Cardinal, to hear a sentence whence there shall be none appeal. What wouldst thou in that day that thou hadst done in this? As thou wilt wish thou hadst done then, do now."

"I—can't," faltered the unhappy waverer.

"I would as lief be scalded and have done with it, Tom, as live in such endless terror of hot water coming nigh me. Depend on it, it should be the lesser suffering in the end."

"There's Gertrude," he suggested in the same tone.

"Leave Gertrude be. They'll not touch her. Gertrude shall be of that religion which is the fashion, to the end of her days—without the Lord turn her—and folks of that mettle need fear no persecution. Nay, Tom, 'tis not Gertrude that holdeth thee back from coming out on the Lord's side. God's side is ever the safest in the end. It is thine own weak heart and weak faith, wherein thou restest, and wilt not seek the strength that can do all things, which God is ready to grant thee but for the asking."

"You are a good woman, Frances," answered her brother, with more feeling than he usually showed, "and I would I were more like you."

"Tarry not there, Tom: go on to 'I would I were more like Christ.' There be wishes that fulfil themselves; and aspirations after God be of that nature. And now, dear brother, I commend thee to God, and to the word of His grace. Be thou strong in the Lord, and in the power of His might!"

They kissed each other for the last time, and Mrs Collenwood stood listening to the slow, heavy step which passed up the stairs and into the bedroom overhead. When Mr Roberts had shut and barred his door, she took up the key, and with a sigh which had reference rather to his future than to her present, went to seek Pandora. Their little packages of immediate necessaries were soon made up. When the clock struck midnight—an hour at which in 1557 everybody was in bed—two well cloaked and hooded women crept out of the low-silled window of the dinning-room, and made their silent and solitary way through the shrubs of the pleasure-ground to the little wicket-gate which opened on the Goudhurst road.

Chapter Twenty Two.

Pots and pans.

Mrs Collenwood unlocked the little wicket, and let herself and Pandora out into the public road. Then she relocked the gate, and after a moment's thought, feeling in the darkness, she hung the key on a bush close to the gate, where it could not be seen from the road. Both ladies carried lanterns, for the omission of this custom would have raised more suspicion than its observance, had they been met by any one, and there were no public street lamps in those days. They were bound first for the little hostelry, called the Nun's Head, in the village of Lamberhurst, where Mrs Collenwood had desired her servant to await her; the landlady of which was known to those in the secret to be one of "the brethren," and was therefore sure to befriend and not betray them, if she guessed the truth. Slowly and painfully they made their way by a circuitous route, to avoid passing through Goudhurst, and Pandora, who was not much accustomed to walking, began to be very tired before half the way was traversed. They had just reached the road again, and were making their way slowly through the ruts and puddles—for English roads at that date were in a state which happily we can do little more than imagine—when they heard the sound of hoofs a little way behind them. Mrs Collenwood laid her hand on Pandora's arm.

"Hide the lantern under thy cloak," she whispered; "and we will creep into this field and 'bide quat under the hedge, till the party shall have passed by."

The advice was put into practice. The hoofs drew near, accompanied by a jingling sound which seemed to come from pottery. It was now near one o'clock. The ladies kept as still as mice. They were not reassured when the sound came to a stand-still, just before the gate of the field where they were hidden, and a man's voice, strange to them, said—

"It was just here I lost the sight of the lanterns. They cannot be far off."

Mrs Collenwood felt Pandora's hand clasp her wrist tight in the darkness.

"Bide a moment, Tom, and I will search in the field," said another voice.

Mrs Collenwood gave all up for lost.

"Mistress Pandora, are you there?" said the voice which had last spoken.

"Aunt Frances, 'tis Mr Hall!" cried Pandora joyfully.

"Ah! I am right glad I have found you," said Roger, as he came up to them. "I have been searching you this hour, being confident, from what I heard, that you would attempt to get away to-night. I pray you to allow of my company."

"In good sooth, Mr Hall, we be right thankful of your good company," answered Mrs Collenwood. "'Tis ill work for two weak women such as we be."

"Truly, my mistress, methinks you must both have lion-like hearts, so much as to think of essaying your escape after this fashion. You will be the safer for my presence. I have here an ass laden with pots and pans, and driven by a good man and true, a Gospeller to boot—one of your own men from the cloth-works, that is ready to guard his master's daughter at the hazard of his life if need be. If you be willing, good my mistress, to sell tins and pitchers in this present need—"

"Use me as you judge best, Master Hall," said Mrs Collenwood heartily. "I am willing to sell tins, or scour them, or anything, the better to elude suspicion."

"Well said. Then my counsel is that we turn right about, and pass straight through Goudhurst, so soon as the dawn shall break. The boldest way is at times the safest."

"But is not that to lose time?"

"To lose time is likewise sometimes to gun it," said Roger, with a smile. "There is one danger, my mistresses, whereof you have not thought. To all that see you as you are, your garb speaks you gentlewomen, and gentlewomen be not wont to be about, in especial unattended, at this hour of the night. If it please you to accept of my poor provision, I have here, bound on the ass, two women's cloaks and hoods of the common sort, such as shall better comport with the selling of pots than silken raiment; and if I may be suffered to roll up the cloaks you bear in like manner, you can shift you back to them when meet is so to do."

"Verily, 'tis passing strange that had never come to my mind!" replied Mrs Collenwood. "Mr Hall, we owe you more thanks than we may lightly speak."

They changed their cloaks, rolling up those they took off, and tying them securely on the donkey, covered by a piece of canvas, with which Roger was provided. The hoods were changed in like manner. The donkey was driven into the field in charge of Tom Hartley, who pulled his forelock to his ladies; and the trio sat down to await daylight.

"And if it like you, my mistresses," added Roger, "if it should please Mistress Collenwood to speak to me by the name of Hodge, and Mistress Pandora by that of father or uncle, methinks we should do well."

"Nay, Mr Hall; but I will call you brother," said Pandora, smiling; "for that is what you truly are, both in the Gospel and in descent from Adam."

In perfect quiet they passed the five hours which elapsed ere the sun rose. As soon as ever the light began to break, Roger led forth the donkey; Tom trudging behind with a stick, and the ladies walked alongside.

Rather to their surprise, Roger took his stand openly in the market place of Goudhurst, where he drove a brisk trade with his pots and pans; Mrs Collenwood taking up the business as if she had been to the manner born, and much to Pandora's admiration.

"Brown pitchers, my mistress? The best have we, be sure. Twopence the dozen, these; but we have cheaper if your honour wish them."

Another time it was, "What lack you, sweet sir? Chafing-dishes, shaving-basins, bowls, goblets, salts? All good and sound—none of your trumpery rubbish!"

And Roger and Tom both lifted up sonorous voices in the cry of—

"Pots and pans! Pots and pa–ans! Chargers, dishes, plates, cups, bowls, por–ring–ers! Come buy, come buy, come buy!"

The articles were good—Roger had seen to that—and they went off quickly. Ladies, country housewives, farmers, substantial yeomen, with their wives and daughters, came up to buy, until the donkey's load was considerably diminished. At length a priest appeared as a customer. Pandora's heart leaped into her mouth; and Mrs Collenwood, as she produced yellow basins for his inspection, was not entirely without her misgivings. But the reverend gentleman's attention seemed concentrated on the yellow basins, of which he bought half-a-dozen for a penny, and desired them to be delivered at the Vicarage. Roger bowed extra low as he assured the priest that the basins should be there, without fail, in an hour, and having now reduced his goods to a load of much smaller dimensions, he intimated that they "might as well be moving forward." The goods having been duly delivered, Roger took the road to Lamberhurst, and they arrived without further misadventure at the Nun's Head, where Mrs Collenwood's servant, Zachary, was on the look-out for them.

To Mrs Collenwood's amusement, Zachary did not recognise her until she addressed him by name; a satisfactory proof that her disguise was sufficient for the purpose. They breakfasted at the Nun's Head, on Canterbury brawn (for which that city was famous) and a chicken pie, and resumed their own attire, but carrying the cloaks of Roger's providing with them, as a resource if necessity should arise.

"Aunt Frances," said Pandora, as they sat at breakfast, "I never thought you could have made so good a tradeswoman. Pray you, how knew you what to say to the folks?"

"Why, child!" answered Mrs Collenwood, laughing, "dost reckon I have never bought a brown pitcher nor a yellow basin, that I should not know what price to ask?"

"Oh, I signified not that so much, Aunt; but—all the talk, and the fashion wherein you addressed you to the work."

"My mother—your grandmother, Dorrie—was used to say to me, 'Whatever thou hast ado with, Frank, put thine heart and thy wits therein.' 'Tis a good rule, and will stand a woman in stead for better things than selling pots."

Zachary had made full provision for his mistress's journey. The horses were ready, and the baggage-mules also. He rode himself before Mrs Collenwood, and an old trustworthy man-servant was to sit in front of Pandora. All was ready for proceeding at half-an-hour's notice, and Mrs Collenwood determined to go on at once.

When it came to the leave-taking, she drew a gold ring from her finger, and gave it to Tom Hartley, with a promise that his master should hear through Roger Hall, so soon as the latter deemed it safe, of the very essential service which he had rendered her. Then she turned to Roger himself.

"But to you, Mr Hall," she said, "how can I give thanks, or in what words clothe them? Verily, I am bankrupt therein, and can only thank you to say I know not how."

"Dear mistress," answered Roger, "have you forgot that 'tis I owe thanks to you, that you seek to magnify my simple act into so great deserving? They that of their kindness cheer my little suffering Christie's lonely life, deserve all the good that I can render them. My little maid prayed me to say unto you both that she sent you her right loving commendations, and that she would pray for your safe journey every day the whilst it should last, and for your safety and good weal afterward. She should miss you both sorely, quoth she; but she would pray God to bless you, and would strive to her utmost to abide by all your good and kindly counsel given unto her."

"Dear little Christie!" said Pandora affectionately. "I pray you, Master Hall, tell her I shall never forget her, and I trust God may grant us to meet again in peace."

"I cast no doubt of that, Mistress Pandora," was the grave answer, "though 'twill be, very like, in a better land than this."

"And I do hope," added she, "that Mistress Benden may ere long be set free."

Roger shook his head.

"I have given up that hope," he said; "yea, well-nigh all hopes, for this lower world."

"There is alway hope where God is," said Mrs Collenwood.

"Truth, my mistress," he replied; "but God is in Heaven, and hope is safest there."

It was nearly eleven o'clock in the morning when the travellers set out from the Nun's Head. Roger Hall stood in the doorway, looking after them, until the last glimpse could no longer be perceived. Then, with a sigh, he turned to Tom Hartley, who stood beside him.

"Come, Tom!" he said, "let us, thou and I, go home and do God's will."

"Ay, master, and let God do His will with us," was the cheery answer.

Then the two men and the donkey set out for Cranbrook.

Chapter Twenty Three.

Cat and mouse.

It was Mr Roberts's custom to go down to the cloth-works every Tuesday—saints' days excepted—and in pursuance of this habit he made his appearance in the counting-house on the morning after the departure of the two ladies. Roger Hall was at his post as usual, waited on his master, gave in his accounts, and received his orders. When the other business was over, Roger said, in the same tone and manner as before—

"Those two parcels of rare goods, master, sent forth yester-even, that you wot of, I saw myself so far as Lamberhurst, and they be in safe hands for the further journey."

Mr Roberts did not at once, as might now be done, ask Roger what he was talking about. The days of Romish ascendency in England were days when everybody knew that if a man's meaning were not simple and apparent, there was probably some reason why he dared not speak too plainly, and it was perilous to ask for an explanation. Mr Roberts looked up into his manager's face, and at once guessed his meaning. He was seriously alarmed to see it. How had Roger Hall become possessed of that dangerous secret, which might bring him to prison if it were known? For the penalty for merely "aiding and abetting" a heretic was "perpetual prison." Those who gave a cup of cold water to one of Christ's little ones did it at the peril of their own liberty.

Let us pause for a moment and try to imagine what that would be to ourselves. Could we run such risks for Christ's sake—knowing that on every hand were spies and enemies who would be only too glad to bring us to ruin, not to speak of those idle gossiping people who do much of the world's mischief, without intending harm? It would be hard work to follow the Master when He took the road to Gethsemane. Only love could do it. Would our love stand that sharp test?

All this passed in a moment. What Mr Roberts said was only—"Good. Well done." Then he bent his head over the accounts again; raising it to say shortly—"Hall, prithee shut yon door; the wind bloweth in cold this morrow." Roger Hall obeyed silently: but a change came over Mr Roberts as soon as the door was shut on possible listening ears. He beckoned Roger to come close to him.

"How wist you?" he whispered.

"Guessed it, Master." It was desirable to cut words as short as possible. "Saw him go up to your house. Thought what should follow."

"You followed them?"

"No; came too late. Searched, and found them in a field near Goudhurst."

A shudder came over Pandora's father at the thought of what might have been, if the priest had been the searcher.

"Any one else know?"

"Tom Hartley—true as steel, Master. Two were needful for my plan. Mistress bade me commend him to you, as he that had done her right good service."

"He shall fare the better for it. And you likewise."

Roger smiled. "I did but my duty, Master."

"How many folks do so much?" asked Mr Roberts, with a sigh. *He* could not have said that. After a moment's thought he added—"Raise Hartley twopence by the week; and take you twenty pounds by the year instead of sixteen as now."

"I thank you, Master," said Roger warmly: "but it was not for that."

"I know—I know!" answered the master, as he held out his hand to clasp that of his manager—a rare and high favour at that time. And then, suddenly, came one of those unexpected, overpowering heart-pourings, which have been said to be scarcely more under the control of the giver than of the recipient. "Hall, I could not have done this thing. How come you to have such strength and courage? Would I had them!"

"Master, I have neither, save as I fetch them from Him that hath. 'I can do all things through Christ that strengtheneth me.'"

"He doth not strengthen me!" moaned the weak man.

"Have you asked Him, Master?" quietly replied the strong one.

Mr Roberts made no answer, and Roger knew that meant a negative. In his heart the master was conscious that he had not asked. He had said multitudinous "paters" and "aves," had repeated "Hail Marys" by the score—all the while half thinking of something else; but never once in his inmost soul had he said to the Lord—"Saviour, I am weak; make me strong." A few minutes' silence, and Mr Roberts turned back to the accounts, half-ashamed that he had allowed that glimpse of his true self to be seen. And Roger Hall said no more, except to God.

The master went home to supper at four o'clock. Ten was then the hour for dinner, four for supper; people who kept late hours made it eleven and five. As Mr Roberts came in sight of his own door, his heart sank down into his shoes. On the door-step stood a black-robed figure which he knew only too well, and which he would gladly have given a handful of gold to know he might have no chance of seeing for a month to come. A faint idea of hiding himself in the shrubs crossed his mind for a moment; but he could not stay there for an indefinite time, and the priest would in all probability wait for him, if it were he whom he meant to see. No, it would be better to go forward and get it over; but it was with a fervid wish that it were over that Mr Roberts went on and deferentially saluted his Rector.

That reverend gentleman thoroughly understood his man. Had it been possible to gauge the human soul with a thermometer, he could have guessed with accuracy how it would read. He met him, not with severity, but with a deep gravity which conveyed the idea that something serious required discussion, and that he earnestly hoped the culprit would be able to clear himself of the charge.

In the hall they were met by Mistress Grena and Gertrude, who had seen them coming, and who came forward, as in duty bound, to show extra respect to their spiritual pastor. The genuine spirituality was more than dubious: but that did not matter. He was a "spiritual person"—though the person was exceedingly unspiritual!

The priest gave a blessing to the ladies with two fingers extended in a style which must require some practice, and at Mistress Grena's request sat down with them to supper. During the meal the conversation was general, though the priest retained his serious aspect of something unpleasant to come. The heavy part of the supper was over, and cheese, with late apples, Malaga raisins, and Jordan almonds, had made their appearance; the ladies prepared to withdraw.

"Mistress Holland," said the Rector, "I beseech you to tarry yet a little season"—adding to Gertrude, "I need not detain you, my daughter."

Gertrude escaped with great satisfaction. "Those two are going to catch it!" she said to herself; "I am glad I am out of it!" Mr Roberts knew sorrowfully that the surmise was woefully true, but he was rather relieved to find that his sister-in-law was "going to catch it" with him. Her presence was a sort of stick for him to lean on.

"My son," said the Rector to Mr Roberts, with an air of sorrowful reluctance to begin a distasteful piece of work, "it troubleth me sorely to do that I must needs do, but necessity hath no law. Remember, I pray you, that as yesterday I called here, desiring to have speech of your youngest daughter, and was told by Osmund your butler that she was visiting a friend."

"That was fully truth, Father," said Mistress Grena, as if she supposed that the Rector was about to complain of some duplicity on the part of Osmund.

Mr Bastian waved aside the assurance.

"I left word," he continued, repeating the words with emphasis, "*I left word* that I would call to see her this morrow. Here am I; and what have I now learned? That she left this house yester-even, without so much as a word of excuse, not to say a beseechment of pardon, when she knew that I purposed having speech of her." His voice became more stern. "Is this the manner wherein ye deal with the ministers of holy Church? Truly, had I just cause to suspect your fidelity to her, this were enough to proceed on. But trusting ye may yet have ability to plead your excuse"—a slightly more suave tone was allowed to soften the voice—"I wait to hear it, ere I take steps that were molestous to you, and truly unwelcome unto me. What say ye in extenuation thereof?"

"We are verily sorry, Father," came quietly from Mistress Grena, "that no meet apology hath been offered unto you for this discourtesy, and we pray you of your grace and goodness right gentilly to accept the same even now. Truly the matter stands thus: Our sister, Mistress Collenwood, had in purpose to tarry with us divers days longer; but yester-even tidings came unto her the which caused her to hasten her departure, not tarrying so much as one night more; and as she had desired to take Pandora withal, it was needful that her departure should be hastened likewise. You wot well, good Father, I am assured, the bustle and business caused by such sudden resolve, and the little time left for thought therein: but for any consequent lack of respect unto yourself and your holy office, we are full sorry, and do right humbly entreat you of pardon."

Mr Roberts breathed more freely. He thought the woman's wit was about to prevail, and to salve over the offence.

The priest, on his part, perceived with regret that he had made a mistake in retaining Mistress Grena. Her representations were very plausible, and she was not so easily cowed as her brother-in-law. He considered a moment how to proceed.

"In truth, my daughter," he said, addressing her, "you have fully made your excuse, and I allow it right gladly. I may well conceive that in the haste and labour of making ready on so sudden summons, both you and your niece may easily have forgat the matter. I need not keep you longer from your household duties. God grant you a good even!"

Mistress Grena had no resource but to withdraw in answer to this dismissal, her heart filled with sore forebodings. She had hoped the excuse might be held to cover the whole family; but it was evident the priest had no intention of accepting it as including the male portion thereof. As she passed Mr Roberts, with her back to the priest, she gave him a warning look; but her hope that he would take the warning was as small as it could well be.

"And now, my son," said the Rector softly, turning to his remaining victim, "how say you? Were you likewise busied in preparing the gentlewomen for their journey?"

Chapter Twenty Four.

Counterplot.

A man to be very much pitied was poor Mr Roberts. Not only had he to pacify the priest, but Mistress Grena's line of defence, plausible as it sounded, had unhappily crossed and invalidated the excuse he had intended to make for himself. His faint, hazy purpose up to that time had been to deny any knowledge of the escape; but after it had been thus represented as a natural, every-day occurrence, how was he to keep up the story? Yet he had no other ready.

"No, Father—ay, it—I was a-bed," was his blundering reply.

The priest's voice was sweet as a newly-tuned piano.

"Was it not strange, my son, that you heard no sounds from beneath? Or went you up, knowing what was passing?"

What was the poor man to do? If he acknowledged that he knew of the escape of the fugitives, he laid himself open to the charge of "aiding and abetting"; if he denied it, he practically denied also the truth of Grena's defence. At that moment he would have given every acre and shilling in his possession to be free from this horrible cross-questioning.

The cat watched the poor mouse wriggle with grim satisfaction. Either way, it would come to its claws at last.

Suddenly the scene of the morning was reproduced to the mind's eye of the tortured man. Roger Hall's voice seemed to say again—"Have you asked Him, Master?" Faintly, tremblingly in the unwontedness of the act, the request was made, and even that slight contact with the unchanging Rock steadied the wavering feet. He must speak truth, and uphold Grena.

"Father," he said in a changed tone, "my sister told you true. The journey was hastened, and that suddenly."

The change in his tone puzzled the priest. What had come to the man, in that momentary interval, to nerve him thus anew?

"How came the news, my son?"

Mr Roberts was thankfully able to answer that he knew not.

"But surely, with so much baggage as Mistress Collenwood must have borne withal, the number of horses that left your house could not but be noted of them in the vicinage. Yet I am told no sound was heard."

"My sister sent the most part of her baggage away before her," was the answer.

"Remember," said the Rector sternly, "the sin you incur if you deceive a priest!"

"I have not spoken one untrue word, Father."

At that moment the door-bell was rung, and answered by Osmund, who, coming into the room, deferentially informed the priest that my Lord Cardinal had sent his sumner to the Rectory, with a command that he, Mr Bastian, should attend his court at eight o'clock on the following morning. The interruption was welcome to both parties. The priest was perplexed, and wanted time to think, no less than Mr Roberts. He had anticipated an easy victory, and found himself unaccountably baffled.

In the present day, no English gentleman would bear such questioning by a priest. The latter would very soon be told, in however civil language, that an Englishman's house was his castle, and that he held himself responsible for his actions to God alone. But the iron terror of Rome was then over every heart. No priest could be defied, nor his questions evaded, with impunity. If those days ever come back, it will be the fault and the misery of Englishmen who would not take warning by the past, but who suffered the enemy to creep in again "while men slept." The liberties of England, let us never forget, were bought with the blood of the Marian martyrs.

No sooner had the priest departed than Mistress Grena silently slid into the room. She had evidently been on the watch.

"Brother," she said, in a voice which trembled with doubt and fear, "what have you told him?"

"What you told him, Grena."

"Oh!" The exclamation spoke of intense relief.

"But you may thank Roger Hall for it."

"Roger Hall!—what ado had he therewith?"

"If you ask at him," answered Mr Roberts with a smile, "methinks he will scarce know."

"Will he come again?" she asked fearfully—not alluding to Roger Hall.

"I wis not. Very like he will—maybe till he have consumed us. Grena, I know not how it hath been with you, but for me, I have been an arrant coward. God aiding me, I will be thus no longer, but will go forth in the strength of the Lord God. Believe you these lying wonders and deceitful doctrines? for I do not, and have never so done, though I have made believe to do it. I will make believe no longer. I will be a man, and no more a puppet, to be moved at the priest's pleasure. Thank God, Pan is safe, and Gertrude is not like to fall in trouble. How say you? Go you with me, or keep you Gertrude's company?"

Then Grena Holland broke down. All her little prim preciseness vanished, and the real woman she was came out of her shell and showed herself.

"O Tom!" she said, sobbing till she could hardly speak: for when restrained, self-contained natures like hers break down, they often do it utterly. "O Tom! God bless thee, and help me to keep by thee, and both of us to be faithful to the end! I too have sinned and done foolishly, and set evil ensample. Forgive me, my brother, and God forgive us both!"

Mr Roberts passed his arm round her, and gave her the kiss of peace.

"Methinks we had best forgive each the other, Grena; and I say Amen to thy 'God forgive us both!'"

When Mr Bastian arrived at Canterbury a little after daybreak the next morning, he found, as he had expected, that while the message had been sent in the name of Cardinal Pole, it was really the Bishop of Dover who required his attendance. The Bishop wanted to talk with the parish priest concerning the accused persons from his parish. He read their names from a paper whereon he had them noted down—"John Fishcock, butcher; Nicholas White, ironmonger; Nicholas Pardue, cloth-worker; Alice Benden, gentlewoman; Barbara Final, widow, innkeeper; Sens Bradbridge, widow; Emmet Wilson, cloth-worker's wife."

"Touching Alice Benden," said the Bishop, "I require no note at your hands; I have divers times spoken with her, and know her to be a right obstinate heretic, glorying in her errors. 'Tis the other concerning whom I would have some discourse with you. First, this John Fishcock, the butcher: is he like to be persuaded or no?"

"Methinks, nay, my Lord: yet am I not so full sure of him as of some other. The two Nicholases, trow, are surer of the twain. You should as soon shake an ancient oak as White; and Pardue, though he be a man of few words, is of stubborn conditions."

"Those men of few words oft-times are thus. And how for the women, Brother? Barbara Final—what is she?"

"A pleasant, well-humoured, kindly fashion of woman; yet methinks not one to be readily moved."

"Sens Bradbridge?"

"A poor creature—weakly, with few wits. I should say she were most like of any to recant, save that she hath so little wit, it were scarce to our credit if she so did."

The Bishop laughed. "Emmet Wilson?"

"A plain woman, past middle age, of small learning, yet good wit by nature. You shall not move her, holy Father, or I mistake."

"These heretics, what labour they give us!" said Dick of Dover, rather testily. "'Tis passing strange they cannot conform and have done with it, and be content to enjoy their lives and liberties in peace."

Having no principle himself, the Bishop was unable to comprehend its existence in other people. Mr Bastian was a shade wiser—not that he possessed much principle, but that he could realise the fact of its existence.

"There is one other point, holy Father," said he, seeing that the Bishop was about to dismiss him, "whereon, if it stand with your Lordship's pleasure, I would humbly seek your counsel."

The Bishop rubbed his hands, and desired Mr Bastian to proceed. The labour which the heretics gave him was very well to complain of, but to him the excitement of discovering a new heretic was as pleasurable as the unearthing of a fox to a keen sportsman. Dick of Dover, having no distinct religious convictions, was not more actuated by personal enmity to the persecuted heretic than the sportsman to the persecuted fox. They both liked the run, the excitement, the risks, and the glory of the sport.

"To tell truth, my Lord," continued Mr Bastian, dropping his voice, "I am concerned touching a certain parishioner of mine, a gentleman, I am sorry to say, of name and ancient family, cousin unto Mr Roberts of Glassenbury, whose name you well know as one of the oldest houses in Kent."

The Bishop nodded assent.

"'Tis true, during King Edward's time, he went for one of the new learning; but he conformed when the Queen came in, and ever sithence have I regarded him as a good Catholic enough, till of late, when I am fallen to doubt it, to my great concern." And Mr Bastian proceeded to relate to the Bishop all that he knew respecting the flight of the ladies, and his subsequent unsatisfactory interview with the heads of the family. The Bishop listened intently.

"This young maid," said he, when the narrative was finished, "what said you was her name—Gertrude?—this Gertrude, then, you account of as faithful to holy Church?"

"She hath ever been regular at mass and confession, my Lord, and performeth all her duties well enough. For other matter, methinks, she is somewhat light-minded, and one that should cast more thought to the colour of her sleeves than to the length of her prayers."

"None the worse for that," said Dick of Dover—adding hastily, as the unclerical character of his remark struck him—"for this purpose, of course, I signify; for this purpose. Make you a decoy of her, Brother, to catch the other."

"I cry your Lordship mercy, but I scarce take you. Her father and aunt do come to confession—somewhat irregularly, 'tis true; but they do come; and though the woman be cautious and wily, and can baffle my questions if she will, yet is the man transparent as glass, and timid as an hare. At least, he hath been so until this time; what turned him I wis not, but I am in hopes it shall not last."

"Move this girl Gertrude to listen behind the arras, when as they talk together," suggested the Bishop. "Make her promises—of anything she valueth, a fine horse, a velvet gown, a rich husband—whatever shall be most like to catch her."

Mr Bastian smiled grimly, as he began to see the plot develop.

"'Tis an easy matter to beguile a woman," said the Bishop, who, being very ignorant of women, believed what he said: "bait but your trap with something fine enough, and they shall walk in by shoals like herrings. Saving these few obstinate simpletons such as Alice Benden, that you can do nought with, they be light enough fish to catch. Catch Gertrude, Brother."

Chapter Twenty Five.

Before Dick of Dover.

"Perkins!" said a rather pompous voice.

Perkins was the Cathedral bell-ringer, and the gaoler of Alice Benden. He obeyed the summons of the pompous voice with obsequious celerity, for it belonged to no less a person than the Lord Bishop of Dover. His Lordship, having caught sight of the bell-ringer as he crossed the precincts, had called him, and Perkins came up, his hat in one hand, and pulling his forelock with the other.

"I desire to know, Perkins," said the Bishop, "if that man that is your prisoner's brother hath yet been arrested, as I bade?"

"Well, nay, my Lord, he haven't," said Perkins, his heart fluttering and his grammar questionable.

"And wherefore no?" asked the Bishop sternly.

"Well, my Lord, truth is, I haven't chanced on him since."

"He hath not visited his sister, then?"

"Well," answered Perkins, who seemed to find that word a comfort, "ay, he have; but him and me, we hasn't been at same time, not yet."

"Call you that diligence in the keeping of your prisoner?"

"Please your Lordship, she's there, all safe."

"I bade you arrest *him*," insisted the Bishop.

Perkins chewed a sprig of dried lavender, and kept silence.

"I am sore displeased with you, Perkins!"

Perkins looked provokingly obtuse. If the Bishop had only known it, he was afraid of vexing him further by saying anything, and accordingly he said nothing.

"Keep diligent watch for the man, and seize him when he cometh again. As for the woman, bring her before me to-morrow at nine o' the clock. Be careful what you do, as you value my favour."

Perkins pulled his forelock again, and departed.

"The man is hard as a stone," said the Bishop to one of the Canons, with whom he was walking: "no impression can be made upon him."

"He is scantly the worse gaoler for that, under your Lordship's correction," said the Canon carelessly.

"He makes an hard keeper, I cast no doubt," answered the Bishop.

Perkins's demeanour changed as soon as his Lordship had passed out of sight and hearing.

"Dick o' Dover's in a jolly fume!" he said to one of the vergers whom he met.

"Why, what's angered him?"

"I have, belike, that I catched not yon man, Mistress Benden's brother, a-coming to see her. Why, the loon's full o' wiles—never comes at after sunrise. It'd take an eel to catch him. And I'm not his thief-catcher, neither. I works hard enough without that. Old Dick may catch his eels his self if he lacks 'em."

"Work 'll never kill thee, Jack Perkins," replied the verger, with a laugh. "Thou'dst best not get across with Dick o' Dover; he's an ugly customer when he's in the mind."

The right reverend prelate to whom allusion was thus unceremoniously made, was already seated on his judgment bench when, at nine o'clock the next morning, Perkins threw open the door of Monday's Hole.

"Come forth, Mistress; you're to come afore the Bishop."

"You must needs help me up, then, for I cannot walk," said Alice Benden faintly.

Perkins seized her by the arm, and dragged her up from the straw on which she was lying. Alice was unable to repress a slight moan.

"Let be," she panted; "I will essay to go by myself; only it putteth me to so great pain."

With one hand resting on the wall, she crept to the door, and out into the passage beyond. Again Perkins seized her—this time by the shoulder.

"You must make better speed than this, Mistress," he said roughly. "Will you keep the Lord Bishop a-waiting?"

Partly limping by herself, partly pulled along by Perkins, and at the cost of exquisite suffering, for she was crippled by rheumatism, Alice reached the hall wherein the Bishop sat. He received her in the suavest manner.

"Now, my good daughter, I trust your lesson, which it was needful to make sharp, hath been well learned during these weeks ye have had time for meditation. Will you now go home, and go to church, and conform you to the Catholic religion as it now is in England? If you will do this, we will gladly show you all manner of favour; ye shall be our white child, I promise you, and any requests ye may prefer unto us shall have good heed. Consider, I pray you, into what evil case your obstinacy hath hitherto brought you, and how blissful life ye might lead if ye would but renounce your womanish opinions, and be of the number of the Catholics. Now, my daughter, what say you?"

Then Alice Benden lifted her head and answered.

"I am thoroughly persuaded, by the great extremity that you have already showed me, that you are not of God, neither can your doings be godly; and I see that you seek mine utter destruction. Behold, I pray you, how lame I am of cold taken, and lack of food, in that painful prison wherein I have lain now these nine weary weeks, that I am not able to move without great pain."

"You shall find us right different unto you, if you will but conform," replied the Bishop, who, as John Bunyan has it, had "now all besugared his lips."

"Find you as it list you, I will have none ado with you!" answered the prisoner sturdily.

But at that moment, trying to turn round, the pain was so acute that it brought the tears to her eyes, and a groan of anguish to her lips. The Bishop's brows were compressed.

"Take her to West Gate," he said hastily. "Let her be clean kept, and see a physician if she have need."

The gaoler of West Gate was no brutal, selfish Perkins, but a man who used his prisoners humanely. Here Alice once again slept on a bed, was furnished with decent clean clothing and sufficient food. But such was the effect of her previous suffering, that after a short time, we are told, her skin peeled off as if she had been poisoned.

One trouble Alice had in her new prison—that she must now be deprived of Roger's visits. She was not even able to let him know of the change. But Roger speedily discovered it, and it was only thanks to the indolence of Mr Perkins, who was warm in bed, and greatly indisposed to turn out of it, that he was not found out and seized on that occasion. Once more he had to search for his sister. No secret was made of the matter this time; and by a few cautious inquiries Roger discovered that she had been removed to West Gate. His hopes sprang up on hearing it, not only because, as he knew, she would suffer much less in the present, but also because he fondly trusted that it hinted at a possibility of release in the future. It was with a joyful heart that he carried the news home to Christabel, and found her Aunt Tabitha sitting with her.

"O Father, how delightsome!" cried Christie, clapping her hands. "Now if those ill men will only let dear Aunt Alice come home—"

"When the sky falleth, we may catch many larks," said Tabitha, in her usual grim fashion. "Have you told him?"

"Whom?—Edward Benden? No, I'm in no haste to go near him."

"I would, if I knew it should vex him."

"Tabitha!" said Roger, with gentle reproval.

"Roger Hall, if you'd had to stand up to King Ahab, you'd have made a downright poor Elijah!"

"Very like, Tabitha. I dare say you'd have done better."

"Father," said Christie, "did you hear what should come of Master White, and Mistress Final, and all the rest."

"No, my dear heart: I could hear nought, save only that they were had up afore my Lord of Dover, and that he was very round with them, but all they stood firm."

"What, Sens Bradbridge and all?" said Tabitha. "I'd have gone bail that poor sely hare should have cried off at the first shot of Dick o' Dover's arrow. Stood *she* firm, trow?"

"All of them, I heard. Why, Tabitha, the Lord's grace could hold up Sens Bradbridge as well as Tabitha Hall."

"There'd be a vast sight more wanted, I promise you!" said Tabitha self-righteously. "There isn't a poorer creature in all this 'varsal world, nor one with fewer wits in her head than Sens Bradbridge. I marvel how Benedick stood her; but, dear heart! men are that stupid! Christie, don't you never go to marry a man. I'll cut you off with a shilling an' you do."

"Cut me off what, Aunt Tabitha?" inquired Christie, with some alarm in her tone.

"Off my good-will and favour, child."

"Thank you, Aunt Tabitha, for telling me I didn't know I was on," said Christie simply.

"Good lack!" exclaimed Tabitha, in a tone which was a mixture of amusement and annoyance. "Did the child think I cared nought about her, forsooth?"

"O Aunt Tabitha, do you?" demanded Christie, in a voice of innocent astonishment. "I am so glad. Look you, whenever you come, you always find fault with me for something, so I thought you didn't."

"Bless the babe! Dost think I should take all that trouble to amend thee, if I loved thee not?"

"Well, perhaps—" said Christie hesitatingly.

"But Aunt Alice always tried to mend me, and so does Father: but somehow they don't do it like you, Aunt Tabitha."

"They're both a deal too soft and sleek with thee," growled Aunt Tabitha. "There's nought 'll mend a child like a good rattling scolding, without 'tis a thrashing, and thou never hast neither."

"Art avised (are you sure) o' that, Tabitha?" asked Roger. "God sends not all His rain in thunderstorms."

"Mayhap not; but He does send thunderstorms, and earthquakes too," returned Tabitha triumphantly.

"I grant you; but the thunderstorms are rare, and the earthquakes yet rarer; and the soft dew cometh every night. And 'tis the dew and the still small rain, not the earthquakes, that maketh the trees and flowers to grow."

"Ah, well, you're mighty wise, I cast no doubt," answered Tabitha, getting up to go home. "But I tell you I was well thrashed, and scolded to boot, and it made a woman of me."

"I suppose, Father," said Christie, when Tabitha had taken her departure, "that the scolding and beating did make a woman of Aunt Tabitha; but please don't be angry if I say that it wasn't as pleasant a woman as Aunt Alice."

Chapter Twenty Six.

"A ruck of trouble."

"Well, be sure! if there ever was a woman in such a ruck of trouble!" said poor Collet Pardue, wiping her eyes. "Here's my man took to prison, saints knows what for—my man 'at was as quiet as ever a mouse, and as good to me as if he'd ha' been a cherubim, and me left with all them childre—six lads and four lasses—eight o' my own, and two of poor Sens's—and the lads that mischievous as I scarce knows whether I'm on my head or my heels one half o' the day! Here's that Silas a-been and took and dropped the bucket down the well, and never a drop o' water can we get. And Aphabell he's left the gate open, and nine out o' my fourteen chicken strayed away. And I sent Toby for a loaf o' biscuit-bread, a-thinking it'd be a treat for the little uns, and me not having a mite o' time to make it—and if the rogue hasn't been and ate it all up a-coming home—there's the crumbs on his jacket this minute!"

"I didn't!" shouted Tobias resentfully, in answer to this unjust accusation. "I didn't eat it all up! I gave half on it to Esdras—a good half." The last words were uttered in a tone of conscious virtue, the young gentleman evidently feeling that his self-denial was not meeting its due reward.

"Ha' done then, thou runagate!" returned his mother, aiming a slap at him, which Tobias dodged by a dip of his head. "Eh, deary me, but they are a weary lot, these childre!"

"Why stand you not up to them better, Collet Pardue?" asked the neighbour who was the listener to poor Collet's list of grievances. "Can't you rouse yourself and see to them?"

"Seems to me, Mistress Hall, I've got no rouse left in me, wi' all these troubles a-coming so thick," said poor Collet, shaking her head. "If you'd six lads and four maids, and your man in prison for nought, and the bucket down the well, and the chicken strayed, and your poor old mother sick a-bed, and them pies in the oven a-burning this minute—Oh me!"

Collet made a rush at the oven, having to push Charity Bradbridge out of her way, who was staring open-mouthed at the brilliant parrot wrought in floss silks on the exterior of Mrs Tabitha's large work-bag.

"I've told you twenty times, Collet Pardue, you lack method," pursued Mrs Hall, with a magisterial air. "Why set you not Esdras to hunt the chicken, and Noah to fish up the bucket, and Beatrice to wait on your mother, and Penuel to see to the pies, and leave yourself freer? I make my childre useful, I can tell you. The more children, the more to wait on you."

"Well, Mistress Hall, I've always found it t'other way about—the more childre, the more for you to wait on. Pen, she's ironing, and Beatie is up wi' mother. But as to Esdras hunting up the chicks, why, he'd come home wi' more holes than he's got, and that's five, as I know to my cost; and set Noah to get up the bucket, he'd never do nought but send his self a-flying after it down the well, and then I should have to fish him up. 'Tis mighty good talking, when you've only three, and them all maids; maids can be ruled by times; but them lads, they're that cantankerous as— There now, I might ha' known Noah was after some mischief; he's never quiet but he is! Do 'ee look, how he's tangled my blue yarn 'at I'd wound only last night—twisted it round every chair and table in the place, and— You wicked, sinful boy, to go and tangle the poor cat along with 'em! I'll be after you, see if I'm not! You'll catch some'at!"

"Got to catch me first!" said Noah, with a grin, darting out of the door as his over-worried mother made a grab at him.

Poor Collet sat down and succumbed under her sufferings, throwing her apron over her face for a good cry. Beatrice, who came down the ladder which led to the upper chambers, took in the scene at a glance. She was a bright little girl of ten years old. Setting down the tray in her hand, she first speedily delivered the captive pussy, and then proceeded deftly to disentangle the wool, rolling it up again in a ball.

"Prithee, weep not, Mother, dear heart!" she said cheerily. "Granny sleeps, and needs no tending at this present. I've set pussy free, I shall soon have the yarn right again. You're over-wrought, poor Mother!"

Her child's sympathetic words seemed to have the effect of making Collet cry the harder; but Tabitha's voice responded for her.

"Well said, Beatrice, and well done! I love to see a maid whose fingers are not all thumbs. But, dear me, Collet, what a shiftless woman are you! Can't you pack those lads out o' door, and have a quiet house for your work? I should, for sure!"

"You'd find you'd got your work cut out, Mistress Hall, I can tell you. 'Pack 'em out o' door' means just send 'em to prey on your neighbours, and have half-a-dozen angry folks at you afore night, and a sight o' damage for to pay."

"Set them to weed your garden, can't you? and tie up that trailing honeysuckle o'er the porch, that's a shame to be seen. Make 'em useful—that's what I say."

"And 'tis what I'd be main thankful to do if I could—that I'll warrant you, Mistress Hall; but without I stood o'er 'em every minute of the time, the flowers 'd get plucked up and the weeds left, every one on 'em. That'd be useful, wouldn't it?"

"You've brought them up ill, Collet, or they'd be better lads than that. I'd have had 'em as quat as mice, the whole six, afore I'd been their mother a week."

"I cast no doubt, Mistress Hall," said Collet, driven to retort as she rarely did, "if you'd had the world to make, it'd ha' been mortal grand, and all turned out spic-span: look you, the old saw saith, 'Bachelors' wives be always well-learned,' and your lads be angels, that's sure, seein' you haven't ne'er a one on 'em; but mine isn't so easy to manage as yourn, looking as I've six to see to."

"You've lost your temper, Collet Pardue," said Mrs Tabitha, with calm complacency; "and that's a thing a woman shouldn't do who calls herself a Christian."

Before Collet could reply, a third person stood in the doorway. She looked up, and saw her landlord, Mr Benden.

As it happened, that gentleman was not aware of the presence of his sister-in-law, who was concealed from him by the open door behind which she was sitting, as well as by a sheet which was hanging up to air in the warm atmosphere of the kitchen. He had not, therefore, the least idea that Tabitha heard his words addressed to Collet.

"So your husband has been sent to prison, Mistress, for an heretic and a contemner of the blessed Sacrament?"

"My husband contemns not the blessed Sacrament that our Lord Jesus Christ instituted," answered Collet, turning to face her new assailant; "but he is one of them that will not be made to commit idolatry unto a piece of bread."

"Well said, indeed!" sneered Mr Benden. "This must needs be good world when cloth-workers' wives turn doctors of religion! How look you to make my rent, Mistress, with nought coming in, I pray you?"

"Your rent's not due, Master, for five weeks to come."

"And when they be come, I do you to wit, I will have it—or else forth you go. Do you hear, Mistress Glib-tongue?"

"Dear heart, Master Benden!" cried Collet, in consternation. "Sure you can never have the heart to turn us adrift—us as has always paid you every farthing up to the hour it was due!"

"Ay, and I'll have this, every farthing up to the hour 'tis due! I'll have no canting hypocrites in my houses, nor no such as be notorious traitors to God and the Queen's Majesty! I'll—"

"O Master, we're no such, nor never was—" began the sobbing Collet.

But both speeches were cut across by a third voice, which made the landlord turn a shade paler and stop his diatribe suddenly; for it was the voice of the only mortal creature whom Edward Benden feared.

"Then you'd best turn yourself out, Edward Benden, and that pretty sharp, before I come and make you!" said the unexpected voice of the invisible Tabitha. "I haven't forgot, if you have, what a loyal subject you were in King Edward's days, nor how you essayed to make your court to my Lord of Northumberland that was, by proclaiming my Lady Jane at Cranbrook, and then, as soon as ever you saw how the game was going, you turned coat and threw up your cap for Queen Mary. If all the canting hypocrites be bundled forth of Staplehurst, you'll be amongst the first half-dozen, I'll be bound! Get you gone, if you've any shame left, and forbear to torture an honest woman that hath troubles enow."

"He's gone, Mistress Hall," said little Beatrice. "I count he scarce heard what you last spake."

"O Mistress Hall, you are a good friend, and I'm for ever bounden to you!" said poor Collet, when she was able to speak for tears. "And if it please you, I'm main sorry I lost my temper, and if I said any word to you as I shouldn't, I'll take 'em back every one, and may God bless you!"

"Well said, old friend!" answered Tabitha, in high good-humour.

"And, O Mistress, do you think, an' it like you, that Master Benden will turn us forth on Saint Austin's morrow?—that's when our rent's due."

"What is your rent, neighbour?"

"'Tis thirteen-and-fourpence, the house, Mistress—but then we've the bit o' pasture land behind, for our horse and cow—that's eight shillings more by the year. And I've only"—Collet went to a chest, and lifted out an old black stocking—"I haven't but sixteen shillings laid by towards it, and look you, there'll be no wages coming in save Toby's and Esdras' and Aphabell's, and we've to live. With 'leven of us to eat and be clad, we can't save many pence for rent, and I did hope Master Benden 'd be pleased to wait a while. Of course he must have his own, like any other; but if he would ha' waited—"

"He'll wait," said Tabitha, and shut her mouth with a snap. "But lest he should not, Collet, come by Seven Roads as you go to pay your rent, and whatso you may be short for the full amount, I'll find you."

"Eh dear, Mistress Hall, I could cut my tongue in leches (slices) that it ever spake a word as didn't please you!" cried the grateful Collet, though Tabitha had spoken a multitude of words which were by no means pleasing to her. "And we'll all pray God bless you when we're on our knees to-night, and all your folks belike. And I *will* essay to keep the lads better-way, though in very deed I don't know how," concluded she, as Tabitha rose, well pleased, patted Charity on the head, told Beatrice to be a good maid and help her mother, and in a mood divided between gratification and grim plans for giving Mr Benden the due reward of his deeds, set out on her walk home.

Chapter Twenty Seven.

Company in distress.

"Now then, stir up, Mistress Benden! You are to be shifted to the Castle."

Alice Benden looked up as the keeper approached her with that news. The words sounded rough, but the tone was not unkind. There was even a slight tinge of pity in it.

What that transfer meant, both the keeper and the prisoner knew. It was the preparatory step to a sentence of death.

All hope for this world died out of the heart of Alice Benden. No more possibility of reconciliation and forgiveness for Edward!—no more loving counsels to Christabel—no more comforting visits from Roger. Instead of them, one awful hour of scarcely imaginable anguish, and then, from His seat on the right hand of God, Christ would rise to receive His faithful witness—the Tree of Life would shade her, and the Water of Life would refresh her, and no more would the sun light upon her, nor any heat: she should be comforted for evermore. The better hope was to be made way for by the extinction of the lower. She lifted up her heart unto the Lord, and said silently within herself the ancient Christian formula of the early Church—

"Amen, Lord Christ!—so let it be."

In a chair, for she was too crippled to walk, Alice was carried by two of the gaoler's men outside the Cathedral precincts. She had not been in the open air for a month. They carried her out eastwards, across Burgate Street (which dates from the days of King Ethelred), down by the city wall, past Saint George's Gate and the Grey Friars, up Sheepshank's Lane, and so to the old Norman Castle, the keep of which is the third largest of Norman keeps in England, and is now, to the glory of all the Huns and Vandals, converted into a gasometer!

In the barbican sat several prisoners in chains, begging their bread. But Alice was borne past this, and up the north-east staircase, from the walls of which looked out at her verses of the Psalms in Hebrew—silent, yet eloquent witnesses of the dispersion and suffering of Judah—and into a small chamber, where she was laid down on a rude bed, merely a frame with sacking and a couple of blankets upon it.

"Nights be cold yet," said the more humane of her two bearers. "The poor soul 'll suffer here, I'm feared."

"She'll be warm enough anon," said the other and more brutal of the pair. "I reckon the faggots be chopped by now that shall warm her."

Alice knew what he meant. He passed out of the door without another word, but the first man lingered to say in a friendly tone—"Good even to you, Mistress!" It was his little cup of cold water to Christ's servant.

"Good even, friend," replied Alice; "and may our Saviour Christ one day say to thee, 'Inasmuch'!"

Yes, she would be warm enough by-and-by. There should be no more pain nor toil, no more tears nor terrors, whither she was going. The King's "Well done, good and faithful servant!" would mark the entrance on a new life from which the former things had passed away.

She lay there alone till the evening, when the gaoler's man brought her supper. It consisted of a flat cake of bread, a bundle of small onions, and a pint of weak ale. As he set it down, he said—"There'll be company for you to-morrow."

"I thank you for showing it to me," said Alice courteously; "pray you, who is it?"

"'Tis a woman from somewhere down your way," he answered, as he went out; "but her name I know not."

Alice's hopes sprang up. She felt cheered by the prospect of the company of any human creature, after her long lonely imprisonment; and it would be a comfort to have somebody who would help her to turn on her bed, which, unaided, it gave her acute pain to do. Beside, there was great reason to expect that her new companion would be a fellow-witness for the truth. Alice earnestly hoped that they would not—whether out of intended torture or mere carelessness—place a criminal with her. Deep down in her heart, almost unacknowledged to herself, lay a further hope. If it should be Rachel Potkin!

Of the apprehension of the batch of prisoners from Staplehurst Alice had heard nothing. She had therefore no reason to imagine that the woman "from somewhere down her way" was likely to be a personal friend. The south-western quarter of Kent was rather too large an area to rouse expectations of that kind.

It was growing dusk on the following evening before the "company" arrived. Alice had sung her evening Psalms—a cheering custom which she had kept up through all the changes and sufferings of her imprisonment—and was beginning to feel rather drowsy when the sound of footsteps roused her, stopping at her door.

"Now, Mistress! here you be!" said the not unpleasant voice of the Castle gaoler.

"Eh, deary me!" answered another voice, which struck Alice's ear as not altogether strange.

"Good even, friend!" she hastened to say.

"Nay, you'd best say 'ill even,' I'm sure," returned the newcomer. "I've ne'er had a good even these many weeks past."

Alice felt certain now that she recognised the voice of an old acquaintance, whom she little expected to behold in those circumstances.

"Why, Sens Bradbridge, is that you?"

"Nay, sure, 'tis never Mistress Benden? Well, I'm as glad to see you again as I can be of aught wi' all these troubles on me. Is't me? Well, I don't justly know whether it be or no; I keep reckoning I shall wake up one o' these days, and find me in the blue bed in my own little chamber at home. Eh deary, Mistress Benden, but this is an ill look-out! So many of us took off all of a blow belike—"

"Have there been more arrests, then, at Staplehurst? Be my brethren taken?"

"Not as I knows of: but a lot of us was catched up all to oncet—Nichol White, ironmonger, and mine hostess of the White Hart, and Emmet Wilson, and Collet Pardue's man, and Fishwick, the flesher, and me. Eh, but you may give thanks you've left no childre behind you! There's my two poor little maids, that I don't so much as know what's come of 'em, or if they've got a bite to eat these hard times! Lack-a-daisy-me! but why they wanted to take a poor widow from her bits of childre, it do beat me, it do!"

"I am sorry for Collet Pardue," said Alice gravely. "But for your maids, Sens, I am sure you may take your heart to you. The neighbours should be safe to see they lack not, be sure."

"I haven't got no heart to take, Mistress Benden—never a whit, believe me. Look you, Mistress Final she had 'em when poor Benedick departed: and now she's took herself. Eh, deary me! but I cannot stay me from weeping when I think on my poor Benedick. He was that staunch, he'd sure ha' been took if he'd ha' lived! It makes my heart fair sore to think on't!"

"Nay, Sens, that is rather a cause for thanksgiving."

"You always was one for thanksgiving, Mistress Benden."

"Surely; I were an ingrate else."

"Well, I may be a nigrate too, though I wis not what it be without 'tis a blackamoor, and I'm not that any way, as I knows: but look you, good Mistress, that's what I alway wasn't. 'Tis all well and good for them as can to sing psalms in dens o' lions; but I'm alway looking for to be ate up. I can't do it, and that's flat."

"The Lord can shut the lions' mouths, Sens."

"Very good, Mistress; but how am I to know as they be shut?"

"'They that trust in the Lord shall not want any good thing.'" A sudden moan escaped Alice's lips just after she had said this, the result of an attempt to move slightly. Sens Bradbridge was on her knees beside her in a moment.

"Why, my dear heart, how's this, now? Be you sick, or what's took you?"

"I was kept nine weeks, Sens, on foul straw, with never a shift of clothes, and no meat save bread and water, the which has brought me to this pass, being so lame of rheumatic pains that I cannot scarce move without moaning."

"Did ever man hear the like! Didn't you trust in the Lord, then, Mistress, an't like you?—or be soft beds and well-dressed meat and clean raiment not good things?"

Alice Benden's bright little laugh struck poor desponding Sens as a very strange thing.

"Maybe a little of both, old friend. Surely there were four sore weeks when I was shut up in Satan's prison, no less than in man's, and I trusted not the Lord as I should have done—"

"Well, forsooth, and no marvel!"

"And as to beds and meat and raiment—well, I suppose they were not good things for me at that time, else should my Father have provided them for me."

Poor Sens shook her head slowly and sorrowfully.

"Nay, now, Mistress Benden, I can't climb up there, nohow.—'Tis a brave place where you be, I cast no doubt, but I shall never get up yonder."

"But you have stood to the truth, Sens?—else should you not have been here."

"Well, Mistress! I can't believe black's white, can I, to get forth o' trouble?—nor I can't deny the Lord, by reason 'tisn't right comfortable to confess Him? But as for comfort—and my poor little maids all alone, wi' never a penny—and my poor dear heart of a man as they'd ha' took, sure as eggs is eggs, if so be he'd been there—why, 'tis enough to crush the heart out of any woman. But I can't speak lies by reason I'm out o' heart."

"Well said, true heart! The Lord is God of the valleys, no less than of the hills; and if thou be sooner overwhelmed by the waters than other, He shall either carry thee through the stream, or make the waters lower when thou comest to cross."

"I would I'd as brave a spirit as yourn, Mistress Benden."

"Thou hast as good a God, Sens, and as strong a Saviour. And mind thou, 'tis the weak and the lambs that He carries; the strong sheep may walk alongside. 'He knoweth our frame,' both of body and soul. Rest thou sure, that if thine heart be true to Him, so long as He sees thou hast need to be borne of Him, He shall not put thee down to stumble by thyself."

"Well!" said Sens, with a long sigh, "I reckon, if I'm left to myself, I sha'n't do nought but stumble. I always was a poor creature; Benedick had to do no end o' matters for me: and I'm poorer than ever now he's gone, so I think the Lord'll scarce forget me; but seems somehow as I can't take no comfort in it."

"'Blessed are the poor in spirit!'" said Alice softly. "The 'God of all comfort,' Sens, is better than all His comforts."

Chapter Twenty Eight.

Behind the arras.

"You had best make up your mind, Grena, whilst you yet may. This may be the last chance to get away hence that you shall have afore—" Mr Roberts hesitated; but his meaning was clear enough. "It doth seem me, now we have this opportunity through Master Laxton's journey, it were well-nigh a sin to miss it. He is a sober, worthy man, and kindly belike; he should take good care of you; and going so nigh to Shardeford, he could drop you well-nigh at your mother's gates. Now I pray you, Grena, be ruled by me, and settle it that you shall go without delay. He cannot wait beyond to-morrow to set forth."

"I grant it all, Tom, and I thank you truly for your brotherly care. But it alway comes to the same end, whensoever I meditate thereon: I cannot leave you and Gertrude."

"But wherefore no, Grena? Surely we should miss your good company, right truly: but to know that you were safe were compensation enough for that. True should be old enough to keep the house—there be many housewives younger—or if no; surely the old servants can go on as they are used, without your oversight. Margery and Osmund, at least—"

"They lack not my oversight, and assuredly not Gertrude's. But you would miss me, Tom: and I could not be happy touching True."

"Wherefore? Why, Grena, you said yourself they should lay no hand on her."

"Nor will they. But Gertrude is one that lacks a woman about her that loveth her, and will yet be firm with her. I cannot leave the child—Paulina's child—to go maybe to an ill end, for the lack of my care and love. She sees not the snares about her heedless feet, and would most likely be tangled in them ere you saw them. Maids lack mothers more than even fathers; and True hath none save me."

"Granted. But for all that, Grena, I would not sacrifice you."

"Tom, if the Lord would have me here, be sure He shall not shut me up in Canterbury Castle. And if He lacks me there, I am ready to go. He will see to you and True in that case."

"But if He lack you at Shardeford, Grena? How if this journey of Mr Laxton be His provision for you, so being?"

There was silence for a moment.

"Ay," said Grena Holland then, "if you and Gertrude go with me. If not, I shall know it is not the Lord's bidding."

"I! I never dreamed thereof."

"Suppose, then, you dream thereof now."

"Were it not running away from duty?"

"Methinks not. 'When they persecute you in one city, flee ye into another,' said our Lord. I see no duty that you have to leave. Were you a Justice of Peace, like your brother, it might be so: but what such have you? But one thing do I see—and you must count the cost, Tom. It may be your estate shall be sequestered, and all your goods taken to the Queen's use. 'Tis perchance a choice betwixt life and liberty on the one hand, and land and movables on the other."

Mr Roberts walked up and down the room, lost in deep thought. It was a hard choice to make: yet "all that a man hath will he give for his life."

"Oh for the days of King Edward the First," he sighed. "Verily, we valued not our blessings whilst we had them."

Grena's look was sympathising; but she left him to think out the question.

"If I lose Primrose Croft," he said meditatively, "the maids will have nought."

"They will have Shardeford when my mother dieth."

"You," he corrected. "You were the elder sister, Grena."

"What is mine is theirs and yours," she said quietly.

"You may wed, Grena."

She gave a little amused laugh. "Methinks, Tom, you may leave that danger out of the question. Shardeford Hall will some day be Gertrude's and Pandora's."

"We had alway thought of it as Pandora's, if it came to the maids, and that Gertrude should have Primrose Croft. But if that go—and 'tis not unlike; in especial if we leave Kent— Grena, I know not what to do for the best."

"Were it not best to ask the Lord, Tom?"

"But how shall I read the answer? Here be no Urim and Thummim to work by."

"I cannot say how. But of one thing am I sure; the Lord never disappointeth nor confoundeth the soul that trusts in Him."

"Well, Grena, let us pray over it, and sleep on it. Perchance we may see what to do for the best by morning light. But one thing I pray you, be ready to go, that there may be no time lost if we decide ay and not nay."

"That will I see to for us all."

Mr Roberts and Grena left the dining-room, where this conversation had been held, shutting the door behind them. She could be heard going upstairs, he into the garden by the back way. For a few seconds there was dead silence in the room; then the arras parted, and a concealed listener came out. In those days rooms were neither papered nor painted. They were either wainscoted high up the wall with panelled wood, or simply white-washed, and large pieces of tapestry hung round on heavy iron hooks. This tapestry was commonly known as arras, from the name of the French town where it was chiefly woven; and behind it, since it stood forward from the wall, was a most convenient place for a spy. The concealed listener came into the middle of the room. Her face worked with conflicting emotions. She stood for a minute, as it were, fighting out a battle with herself. At length she clenched her hand as if the decision were reached, and said aloud and passionately, "I will not!" That conclusion arrived at, she went hastily but softly out of the room, and closed the door noiselessly.

Mistress Grena was very busy in her own room, secretly packing up such articles as she had resolved to take in the event of her journey being made. She had told Margery, the old housekeeper, that she was going to be engaged, and did not wish to be disturbed. If any visitors came Mistress Gertrude could entertain them; and she desired Margery to transmit her commands to that effect to the young lady. That Gertrude herself would interrupt her she had very little fear. They had few tastes and ideas in common. Gertrude would spend the afternoon in the parlour with her embroidery or her virginals—the piano of that time—and was not likely to come near her. This being the case, Mistress Grena was startled and disturbed to hear a rap at her door. Trusting that it was Mr Roberts who wanted her, and who was the only likely person, she went to open it.

"May I come in, Aunt Grena?" said Gertrude.

For a moment Grena hesitated. Then she stepped back and let her niece enter. Her quick, quiet eyes discerned that something was the matter. This was a new Gertrude at her door, a grave, troubled

Gertrude, brought there by something of more importance than usual.

"Well, niece, what is it?"

"Aunt Grena, give me leave for once to speak freely."

"So do, my dear maid."

"You and my father are talking of escape to Shardeford, but you scarce know whether to go or no. Let me tell you, and trust me, for my knowledge is costly matter. Let us go."

Grena stood in amazed consternation. She had said and believed that God would show them what to do, but the very last person in her world through whose lips she expected Him to speak was Gertrude Roberts.

"How—what—who told you? an angel?" she gasped incoherently.

A laugh, short and unmirthful, was the answer.

"Truly, no," said Gertrude. "It was a fallen angel if it were."

"What mean you, niece? This is passing strange!" said Grena, in a troubled tone.

"Aunt, I have a confession to make. Despise me if you will; you cannot so do more than I despise myself. 'Tis ill work despising one's self; but I must, and as penalty for mine evil deeds I am forcing myself to own them to you. You refuse to leave me, for my mother's sake, to go to an ill end; neither will I so leave you."

"When heard you me so to speak, Gertrude?"

"Not an hour since, Aunt Grena."

"You were not present!"

"I was, little as you guessed it. I was behind the arras."

"Wicked, mean, dishonourable girl!" cried Mistress Grena, in a mixture of horror, confusion, and alarm.

"I own it, Aunt Grena," said Gertrude, with a quiet humility which was not natural to her, and which touched Grena against her will. "But hear me out, I pray you, for 'tis of moment to us all that you should so do."

A silent inclination of her aunt's head granted her permission to proceed.

"The last time that I went to shrift, Father Bastian bade me tell him if I knew of a surety that you or my father had any thought to leave Kent. That could not I say, of course, and so much I told him. Then he bade me be diligent and discover the same. 'But after what fashion?' said I; for I do ensure you that his meaning came not into mine head afore he spake it in plain language. When at last I did conceive that he would have me to spy upon you, at the first I was struck with horror. You had so learned me, Aunt Grena, that the bare thought of such a thing was hateful unto me. This methinks he perceived, and he set him to reason with me, that the command of holy Church sanctified the act done for her service, which otherwise had been perchance unmeet to be done. Still I yielded not, and then he told me flat, that without I did this thing he would not grant me absolution of my sins. Then, but not till then, I gave way. I hid me behind the arras this morning, looking that you should come to hold discourse in that chamber where, saving for meat, you knew I was not wont to be. I hated the work no whit less than at the first; but the fear of holy Church bound me. I heard you say, Aunt Grena"—Gertrude's voice softened as Grena had rarely heard it—"that you would not leave Father and me—that you could not be happy touching me—that I had no mother save you, and you would not cast me aside to go to an ill end. I saw that Father reckoned it should be to your own hurt if you tarried. And it struck me to the heart that you should be thinking to serve me the while I was planning how to betray you. Yet if Father Bastian refused to shrive me, what should come of me? And all at once, as I stood there hearkening, a word from the Psalter bolted in upon me, a verse that I mind Mother caused me to learn long time agone: 'I said, I will confess my transgressions unto the Lord; and so Thou forgavest the wickedness of my sin.' Then said I to myself, What need I trouble if the priest will not shrive me, when I can go straight unto the Lord and confess to Him? Then came another verse, as if to answer me, that I wist Father Bastian should have brought forth in like case, 'Whatsoever sins ye retain, they are retained,' and 'Whatsoever ye shall bind on earth shall be bound in heaven.' I could not, I own, all at once see my way through these. They did look to say, 'Unto whom the priest, that is the Church, denieth shrift, the same hath no forgiveness of God.' For a minute I was staggered, till a blind man came to help me up. Aunt Grena, you mind that blind man in the ninth chapter of Saint John's Gospel? He was cast forth of the Church, as the Church was in that day; and it was when our Lord heard that they had cast him forth, that He sought him and bade him believe only on Him, the Son of God. You marvel, Aunt, I may well see, that such meditations as these should come to your foolish maid Gertrude. But I was at a point, and an hard point belike. I had to consider my ways, whether I would or no, when I came to this trackless moor, and wist not which way to go, with a precipice nigh at hand. So now, Aunt Grena, I come to speak truth unto you, and to confess that I have been a wicked maid and a fool; and if you count me no more worth the serving or the saving I have demerited that you should thus account me. Only if so be, I beseech you, save yourself!"

Gertrude's eyes were wet as she turned away.

Grena followed her and drew the girl into her arms.

"My child," she said, "I never held thee so well worth love and care as now. So be it; we will go to Shardeford."

Chapter Twenty Nine.

Whereof the Hero is Jack.

"Ay, we must go, then," said Mr Roberts, with a long-drawn sigh. "This discovery leaves us no choice. For howso God and we may pardon the child, Father Bastian will not so. We must go ere he find it out, and leave Primrose Croft to his fate."

"Father!" exclaimed Gertrude suddenly, "I beseech you, hear me. Uncle Anthony conforms, and he is kindly-hearted as man could wish. If he would come hither, and have a care of Primrose Croft, as though he held it by gift or under lease from you, they should never think to disturb him."

"The maid's wit hath hit the nail on the head!" returned her father, in high satisfaction. "But how shall I give him to know, without letting forth our secret?—and once get it on paper, and it might as well be given to the town crier. 'Walls have ears,' saith the old saw, but paper hath a tongue. And I cannot tell him by word of mouth, sith he is now at Sandwich, and turneth not home afore Thursday. Elsewise that were good counsel."

"Ask True," suggested Mistress Grena with a smile. "The young wit is the readiest amongst us, as methinks."

"Under your correction, Father, could you not write a letter, and entrust it to Margery, to be sent to Uncle as Thursday even—giving it into her hand the last minute afore we depart? Is she not trustworthy, think you?"

"She is trustworthy enough, if she be let be. But I misdoubt if her wits should carry her safe through a discourse with Father Bastian, if he were bent on winning the truth from her. I could trust Osmund better for that; but I looked to take him withal."

"Give me leave then, Father, to walk down to Uncle's, as if I wist not of his absence, and slip the letter into one of his pockets. He alway leaveth one of his gowns a-hanging in the hall."

"And if his Martha were seized with a cleaning fever whilst he is thence, and turned out the pocket, where should we then be? Nay, True, that shall not serve. I can think of no means but that you twain set forth alone—to wit, without me—under guidance of Osmund, and that I follow, going round by Sandwich, having there seen and advertised my brother."

"Were there no danger that way, Tom?"

"There is danger every way," replied Mr Roberts, with a groan. "But maybe there is as little that way as any: and I would fain save Gertrude's inheritance if it may be."

"At the cost of your liberty, Father? Nay, not so, I entreat you!" cried Gertrude, with a flash of that noble nature which seemed to have been awakened in her. "Let mine inheritance go as it will."

"As God wills," gently put in Mistress Grena.

"As God wills," repeated Gertrude: "and keep you safe."

Mistress Grena laid her hand on her brother's shoulder.

"Tom," she said, "let us trust the Lord in this matter. Draw you up, if you will, a lease of Primrose Croft to the Justice, and leave it in the house in some safe place. God can guide his hand to it, if He will. Otherwise, let us leave it be."

That was the course resolved on in the end. It was also decided that they should not attempt to repeat the night escape which had already taken place. They were to set forth openly in daylight, but separately, and on three several pretexts. Mistress Grena was to go on a professed visit to Christabel, old Osmund escorting her; but instead of returning home afterwards, she was to go forward to

Seven Roods, and there await the arrival of Mr Roberts. He was to proceed to his cloth-works at Cranbrook, as he usually did on a Tuesday; and when the time came to return home to supper, was to go to Seven Roods and rejoin Grena. To Gertrude, at her own request, was allotted the hardest and most perilous post of all—to remain quietly at home after her father and aunt had departed, engaged in her usual occupations, until afternoon, when she was to go out as if for a walk, accompanied by the great house-dog, Jack, and meet her party a little beyond Seven Roods. Thence they were to journey to Maidstone and Rochester, whence they could take ship to the North. Jack, in his life-long character of an attached and incorruptible protector, was to go with them. He would be quite as ready, in the interests of his friends, to bite a priest as a layman, and would show his teeth at the Sheriff with as little compunction as at a street-sweeper. Moreover, like all of his race, Jack was a forgiving person. Many a time had Gertrude teased and tormented him for her own amusement, but nobody expected Jack to remember it against her, when he was summoned to protect her from possible enemies. But perhaps the greatest advantage in Jack's guardianship of Gertrude was the fact that there had always been from time immemorial to men—and dogs—an unconquerable aversion, not always tacit, especially on Jack's part, between him and the Rev. Mr Bastian. If there was an individual in the world who might surely be relied on to object to the reverend gentleman's appearance, that individual was Jack: and if any person existed in whose presence Mr Bastian was likely to hesitate about attaching himself to Gertrude's company, that person was Jack also. Jack never had been able to see why the priest should visit his master, and had on several occasions expressed his opinion on that point with much decision and lucidity. If, therefore, Mr Bastian would keep away from the house until Gertrude started on her eventful walk, he was not very likely to trouble her afterwards.

The priest had fully intended to call at Primrose Croft that very afternoon, to see Mr Roberts, or if he were absent, Mistress Grena; but he preferred the gentleman, as being usually more manageable than the lady. He meant to terrify the person whom he might see, by vague hints of something which he had heard—and which was not to be mentioned—that it might be mournfully necessary for him to report to the authorities if more humility and subordination to his orders were not shown. But he was detained, first by a brother priest who wished to consult him in a difficulty, then by the Cardinal's sumner, who brought documents from his Eminence, and lastly by a beggar requesting alms. Having at length freed himself from these interruptions, he set out for Primrose Croft. He had passed through the gates, and was approaching the door, when he saw an unwelcome sight which brought him to a sudden stop. That sight was a long feathery tail, waving above a clump of ferns to the left. Was it possible that the monster was loose? The gate was between Mr Bastian and that tail, in an infinitesimal space of time. Ignorant of the presence of the enemy, the wind being in the wrong direction, Jack finished at leisure his inspection of the ferns, and bounded after Gertrude.

"How exceedingly annoying!" said Mr Bastian to himself. "If that black demon had been out of the way, and safely chained up, as he ought to have been, I could have learned from the girl whether she had overheard anything. I am sure it was her hood that I saw disappearing behind the laurels. How very provoking! It must be Satan that sent the creature this way at this moment. However, she will come to shrift, of course, on Sunday, and then I shall get to know."

So saying, Mr Bastian turned round and went home, Gertrude sauntered leisurely through the garden, went out by the wicket-gate, which Jack preferred to clear at a bound, and walked rather slowly up the road, followed by her sable escort. She was afraid of seeming in haste until she was well out of the immediate neighbourhood. The clouds were so far threatening that she felt it safe to carry her cloak—a very necessary travelling companion in days when there were no umbrellas. She had stitched sundry gold coins and some jewellery into her underclothing, but she could bring away nothing else. John Banks passed her on the road, with a mutual recognition; two disreputable-looking tramps surveyed her covetously, but ventured on no nearer approach when Jack remarked, "If you do—!" The old priest of Cranbrook, riding past—a quiet, kindly old man for whom

Jack entertained no aversion—blessed her in response to her reverence. Two nuns, with inscrutable white marble faces, took no apparent notice of her. A woman with a basket on her arm stopped her to ask the way to Frittenden. Passing them all, she turned away from the road just before reaching Staplehurst, and took the field pathway which led past Seven Roods. Here Jack showed much uneasiness, evidently being aware that some friend of his had taken that way before them, and he decidedly disapproved of Gertrude's turning aside without going up to the house. The path now led through several fields, and across a brook spanned by a little rustic bridge, to the stile where it diverged into the high road from Cranbrook to Maidstone.

As they reached the last field, they saw Tabitha Hall coming to meet them.

"Glad to see you, Mistress Gertrude! All goes well. The Master and Mistress Grena's somewhat beyond, going at foot's pace, and looking out for you. So you won away easy, did you? I reckoned you would."

"Oh, ay, easy enough!" said Gertrude.

But she never knew how near she had been to that which would have made it almost if not wholly impossible.

"But how shall I ride, I marvel?" she asked, half-laughing. "I can scarce sit on my father's saddle behind him."

"Oh, look you, we have a pillion old Mistress Hall was wont to ride on, so Tom took and strapped it on at back of Master's saddle," said Tabitha, with that elaborate carelessness that people assume when they know they have done a kindness, but want to make it appear as small as possible.

"I am truly beholden to you, Mistress Hall; but I must not linger, so I can only pray God be wi' you," said Gertrude, using the phrase which has now become stereotyped into "good-bye."

"But, Mistress Gertrude! won't you step up to the house, and take a snack ere you go further? The fresh butter's but now churned, and eggs new-laid, and—"

"I thank you much, Mistress Hall, but I must not tarry now. May God of His mercy keep you and all yours safe!"

And Gertrude, calling Jack, who was deeply interested in a rabbit-hole, hastened on to the Maidstone Road.

"There's somewhat come over Mistress Gertrude," said Tabitha, as she re-entered her own house. "Never saw her so meek-spoken in all my life. She's not one to be cowed by peril, neither. Friswith, where on earth hast set that big poker? Hast forgot that I keep it handy for Father Bastian and the catchpoll, whichever of 'em lacks it first? Good lack, but I cannot away with that going astray! Fetch it hither this minute. Up in the chamber! Bless me, what could the maid be thinking on? There, set it down in the chimney-corner to keep warm; it'll not take so long to heat then. Well! I trust they'll win away all safe; but I'd as lief not be in their shoon."

A faint sound came from the outside. Jack had spied his friends, and was expressing his supreme delight at having succeeded in once more piecing together the scattered fragments of his treasure.

Chapter Thirty.

Puzzled.

Old Margery Danby, the housekeeper at Primrose Croft, was more thoroughly trustworthy than Mr Roberts had supposed, not only in will—for which he gave her full credit—but in capacity, which he had doubted. Born in the first year of Henry the Seventh, Margery had heard stirring tales in her childhood from parents who had lived through the Wars of the Roses, and she too well remembered Kett's rebellion and the enclosure riots in King Edward's days, not to know that "speech is silvern, but silence is golden." The quiet, observant old woman knew perfectly well that something was "in the wind." It was not her master's wont to look back, and say, "Farewell, Margery!" before he mounted his horse on a Tuesday morning for his weekly visit to the cloth-works; and it was still less usual for Gertrude to remark, "Good-morrow, good Margery!" before she went out for a walk with Jack. Mistress Grena, too, had called her into her own room the night before, and told her she had thought for some time of making her a little present, as a recognition of her long care and fidelity, and had given her two royals—the older name for half-sovereigns. Margery silently "put two and two together," and the result was to convince her that something was about to happen. Nor did she suffer from any serious doubts as to what it was. She superintended the preparation of supper on that eventful day with a settled conviction that nobody would be at home to eat it; and when the hours passed away, and nobody returned, the excitement of Cicely the chamber-maid, and Dick the scullion-boy, was not in the least shared by her. Moreover, she had seen with some amusement Mr Bastian's approach and subsequent retreat, and she expected to see him again ere long. When the bell rang the next morning about eight o'clock, Margery went to answer it herself, and found herself confronting the gentleman she had anticipated.

"Christ save all here!" said the priest, in reply to Margery's reverential curtsey. "Is your master within, good woman?"

"No, Father, an't like you."

"No? He is not wont to go forth thus early. Mistress Grena?"

"No, Sir, nor Mistress Gertrude neither."

The priest lifted his eyebrows. "All hence! whither be they gone?"

"An' it please you, Sir, I know not."

"That is strange. Went they together?"

"No, Sir, separate."

"Said they nought touching their absence?"

"Not to me, Father."

"Have you no fantasy at all whither they went?"

"I took it, Sir, that my master went to the works, as he is wont of a Tuesday; and I thought Mistress Grena was a-visiting some friend. Touching Mistress Gertrude I can say nought."

"She went not forth alone, surely?"

"She took Jack withal, Sir—none else."

The conviction was slowly growing in Mr Bastian's mind that the wave of that feathery tail had deprived him of the only means of communication which he was ever likely to have with Gertrude Roberts. "The sly minx!" he said to himself. Then aloud to Margery, "Do I take you rightly that all they departed yesterday, and have not yet returned?"

"That is sooth, Father."

Margery stood holding the door, with a calm, stolid face, which looked as if an earthquake would neither astonish nor excite her. Mr Bastian took another arrow from his quiver, one which he generally found to do considerable execution.

"Woman," he said sternly, "you know more than you have told me!"

"Father, with all reverence, I know no more than you."

Her eyes met his with no appearance of insincerity.

"Send Osmund to me," he said, walking into the house, and laying down his hat and stick on the settle in the hall.

"Sir, under your good pleasure, Osmund went with Mistress."

"And turned not again?"

"He hath not come back here, Sir."

"Then they have taken flight!" cried the priest in a passion. "Margery Danby, as you fear the judgment of the Church, and value her favour, I bid you tell me whither they are gone."

"Sir, even for holy Church's favour, I cannot say that which I know not."

"On your soul's salvation, do you not know it?" he said solemnly.

"On my soul's salvation, Sir, I know it not."

The priest strode up and down the hall more than once. Then he came and faced Margery, who was now standing beside the wide fireplace in the hall.

"Have you any guess whither your master may be gone, or the gentlewomen?"

"I've guessed a many things since yester-even, Sir," answered Margery quietly, "but which is right and which is wrong I can't tell."

"When Mistress Collenwood and Mistress Pandora went hence secretly in the night-time, knew you thereof, beforehand?"

"Surely no, Father."

"Had you any ado with their departing?"

"The first thing I knew or guessed thereof, Father, was the next morrow, when I came into the hall and saw them not."

Mr Bastian felt baffled on every side. That his prey had eluded him just in time to escape the trap he meant to lay for them, was manifest. What his next step was to be, was not equally clear.

"Well!" he said at last with a disappointed air, "if you know nought, 'tis plain you can tell nought. I must essay to find some that can."

"I have told you all I know, Father," was the calm answer. But Margery did not say that she had told all she thought, nor that if she had known more she would have revealed it.

Mr Bastian took up his hat and stick, pausing for a moment at the door to ask, "Is that black beast come back?"

"Jack is not returned, Sir," answered the housekeeper.

It was with a mingled sense of relief and uneasiness on that point that the priest took the road through the village. That Jack was out of the way was a delicious relief. But suppose Jack should spring suddenly on him out of some hedge, or on turning a corner? Out of the way might turn out to be all the more surely in it.

Undisturbed, however, by any vision of a black face and a feathery tail, Mr Bastian reached Roger Hall's door. Nell opened it, and unwillingly admitted that her master was at home, Mr Bastian being so early that Roger had not yet left his house for the works. Roger received him in his little parlour, to which Christie had not yet been carried.

"Hall, are you aware of your master's flight?"

Roger Hall opened his eyes in genuine amazement.

"No, Sir! Is he gone, then?"

"He never returned home after leaving the works yesterday."

Roger's face expressed nothing but honest concern for his master's welfare. "He left the works scarce past three of the clock," said he, "and took the road toward Primrose Croft. God grant none ill hath befallen him!"

"Nought o' the sort," said the priest bluntly. "The gentlewomen be gone belike, and Osmund with them. 'Tis a concerted plan, not a doubt thereof: and smelleth of the fire (implies heretical opinions), or I mistake greatly. Knew you nought thereof? Have a care how you make answer!"

"Father, you have right well amazed me but to hear it. Most surely I knew nought, saving only that when I returned home yestre'en, my little maid told me Mistress Grena had been so good as to visit her, and had brought her a cake and a posy of flowers from the garden. But if Osmund were with her or no, that did I not hear."

"Was Mistress Grena wont to visit your daughter?"

"By times, Father: not very often."

As all his neighbours must be aware of Mistress Grena's visit, Roger thought it the wisest plan to be perfectly frank on that point.

"Ask at Christabel if she wist whether Osmund came withal."

Roger made the inquiry, and returned with the information that Christabel did not know. From her couch she could only see the horse's ears, and had not noticed who was with it.

"'Tis strange matter," said the priest severely, "that a gentleman of means and station, with his sister, and daughter, and servant, could disappear thus utterly, and none know thereof!"

"It is, Father, in very deed," replied Roger sympathisingly.

"I pray you, Hall, make full inquiry at the works, and give me to wit if aught be known thereof. Remember, you are somewhat under a cloud from your near kinship to Alice Benden, and diligence in this matter may do you a good turn with holy Church."

"Sir, I will make inquiry at the works," was the answer, which did not convey Roger's intention to make no use of the inquiries that could damage his master, nor his settled conviction that no information was to be had.

The only person at all likely to know more than himself was the cashier at the works, since he lived between Cranbrook and Primrose Croft, and Roger carefully timed his inquiries so as not to include him. The result was what he expected—no one could tell him anything. He quickly and diligently communicated this interesting fact to the priest's servant, his master not being at home; and Mr Bastian was more puzzled than ever. The nine days' wonder gradually died down. On the Thursday evening Mr Justice Roberts came home, and was met by the news of his brother's disappearance, with his family. He was so astonished that he sat open-mouthed, knife and spoon in hand, while his favourite dish of broiled fowl grew cold, until he had heard all that Martha had to tell him. Supper was no sooner over, than off he set to Primrose Croft.

"Well, Madge, old woman!" said he to the old housekeeper, who had once been his nurse, "this is strange matter, surely! Is all true that Martha tells me? Be all they gone, and none wist how nor whither?"

"Come in, and sit you down by the fire, Master Anthony," said Margery, in whose heart was a very soft spot for her sometime nursling, "and I'll tell you all I know. Here's the master's keys, they'll maybe be safer in your hands than mine; he didn't leave 'em wi' me, but I went round the house and picked 'em all up, and locked everything away from them prying maids and that young jackanapes of a Dickon. Some he must ha' took with him; but he's left the key of the old press, look you, and that label hanging from it."

The Justice looked at the label, and saw his own name written in his brother's writing.

"Ha! maybe he would have me open the press and search for somewhat. Let us go to his closet, Madge. Thou canst tell me the rest there, while I see what this meaneth."

"There's scarce any rest to tell, Mr Anthony; only they are all gone—Master, and Mistress Grena, and Mistress Gertrude, and Osmund, and bay Philbert, and the black mare, and old Jack."

"What, Jack gone belike! Dear heart alive! Why, Madge, that hath little look of coming again."

"It hasn't, Mr Anthony; and one of Mistress Gertrude's boxes, that she keeps her gems in, lieth open and empty in her chamber."

The Justice whistled softly as he fitted the key in the lock.

Chapter Thirty One.

How he heard it.

"Why, what's this?"

Mr Justice Roberts had opened the old press, tried all the drawers, and come at last to the secret drawer, of whose existence only he and his brother knew. No sooner had he applied his hand to a secret spring, than out darted the drawer, showing that it held a long legal-looking document, and a letter addressed to himself. He opened and read the latter, Margery standing quietly at a little distance. Slowly and thoughtfully, when he had finished the letter, he folded it up, pocketed it, and turned to Margery.

"Ay, Madge," he said, "they are gone."

"And not coming back, Master Anthony?"

"Not while—well, not at this present. Madge, my brother would have me come hither, and take up mine abode here—for a while, look you; and methinks I shall so do."

"Well, Mr Anthony, and I shall be full fain. I've been right trembling in my shoes this three days, lest them noisome pests should think to come and take possession—turn out all. Master's papers, and count Mistress Grena's partlets, and reckon up every crack in the kitchen trenchers; but there's nought 'll keep 'em out, even to you coming, 'cause they'll be a bit 'feared of you, as being a Justice of Peace. Ay, I am glad o' that."

"'Noisome pests'! Why, whom signify you, Madge?"

"Oh, catchpolls, and thirdboroughs (minor constables), and sheriffs, and hangmen, and 'turneys, and the like o' they," replied Margery, not very lucidly: "they be pests, the lot of 'em, as ever I see. They're as ill as plumbers and painters and rats and fleas—once get 'em in, and there's no turning of 'em out. I cannot abide 'em."

Mr Justice Roberts laughed. "Come, Madge, you may as well add 'Justices of Peace'; you've got pretty nigh all else. Prithee look to thy tongue, old woman, or thou shalt find thee indicted for an ill subject unto the Queen. Why, they be her Gracious' servants ('Grace's' was then frequently spelt 'Gracious''), and do her bidding. Thou wouldst not rebel against the Queen's Majesty?"

"I am as true a woman to the Queen's Grace as liveth, Mr Anthony; but them folks isn't the Queen nor the King neither. And they be as cantankerous toads, every one of 'em, as ever jumped in a brook. Do you haste and come, there's a good lad, as you alway was, when you used to toddle about the house, holding by my gown. It'll seem like old times to have you back."

"Well, I can come at once," said the Justice, with a smile at Margery's reminiscences; "for my brother hath left me a power of attorney to deal with his lands and goods; and as he is my landlord, I have but to agree with myself over the leaving of mine house. But I shall bring Martha: I trust you'll not quarrel."

"No fear o' that, Mr Anthony. Martha, she's one of the quiet uns, as neither makes nor meddles; and I've had strife enough to last me the rest o' my life. 'Tis them flaunting young hussies as reckons quarrelling a comfort o' their lives. And now Osmund's hence, Martha can wait on you as she's used, and she and me 'll shake down like a couple o' pigeons."

"Good. Then I'll be hither in a day or twain: and if any of your pests come meantime, you shake my stick at them, Madge, and tell them I'm at hand."

"No fear! I'll see to that!" was the hearty answer.

So the Justice took up his abode at Primrose Croft, and the cantankerous toads did not venture near. Mr Roberts had requested his brother to hold the estate for him, or in the event of his death for Gertrude, until they should return; which, of course, meant, and was quite understood to mean, until the death of the Queen should make way for the accession of the Protestant Princess Elizabeth. Plain speech was often dangerous in those days, and people generally had recourse to some vague form of words which might mean either one thing or another. The Justice went down to the cloth-works on the following Tuesday, and called Roger Hall into the private room.

"Read those, Hall, an' it like you," he said, laying before him Mr Roberts' letter and the power of attorney.

Roger only glanced at them, and then looked up with a smile.

"I looked for something of this kind, Mr Justice," he said. "When Master left the works on Tuesday evening, he said to me, 'If my brother come, Hall, you will see his orders looked to—' and I reckoned it meant somewhat more than an order for grey cloth. We will hold ourselves at your commands, Mr Justice, and I trust you shall find us to your satisfaction."

"No doubt, Hall, no doubt!" replied the easy-tempered Justice. "Shut that further door an instant. Have you heard aught of late touching your sister?"

"Nought different, Mr Justice. She is yet in the Castle, but I cannot hear of any further examination, nor sentence."

"Well, well! 'Tis sore pity folks cannot believe as they should, and keep out of trouble."

Roger Hall was unable to help thinking that if Mr Justice Roberts had spoken his real thoughts, and had dared to do it, what he might have said would rather have been—"'Tis sore pity folks cannot let others alone to believe as they like, and not trouble them."

That afternoon, the Lord Bishop of Dover held his Court in Canterbury Castle, and a string of prisoners were brought up for judgment. Among them came our friends from Staplehurst—Alice Benden, who was helped into Court by her fellow-prisoners, White and Pardue, for she could scarcely walk; Fishcock, Mrs Final, Emmet Wilson, and Sens Bradbridge. For the last time they were asked if they would recant. The same answer came from all—

"By the grace of God, we will not."

Then the awful sentence was passed—to be handed over to the secular arm—the State, which the Church prayed to punish these malefactors according to their merits. By a peculiarly base and hypocritical fiction, it was made to appear that the Church never put any heretic to death—she only handed them over to the State, with a touching request that they might be gently handled! What that gentle handling meant, every man knew. If the State had treated a convicted heretic to any penalty less than death, it would soon have been found out what the Church understood by gentle handling!

Then the second sentence, that of the State, was read by the Sheriff. On Saturday, the nineteenth of June, the condemned criminals were to be taken to the field beyond the Dane John, and in the hollow at the end thereof to be burned at the stake till they were dead, for the safety of the Queen and her realm, and to the glory of God Almighty. God save the Queen!

None of the accused spoke, saving two. Most bowed their heads as if in acceptance of the sentence. Alice Benden, turning to Nicholas Pardue, said with a light in her eyes—

"Then shall we keep our Trinity octave in Heaven!"

Poor Sens Bradbridge, stretching out her arms, cried aloud to the Bishop—"Good my Lord, will you not take and keep Patience and Charity?"

"Nay, by the faith of my body!" was Dick of Dover's reply. "I will meddle with neither of them both."

"His Lordship spake sooth then at the least!" observed one of the amused crowd.

There was one man from Staplehurst among the spectators, and that was John Banks. He debated long with himself on his way home, whether to report the terrible news to the relatives of the condemned prisoners, and at last he decided not to do so. There could be no farewells, he knew, save at the stake itself; and it would spare them terrible pain not to be present. One person, however, he rather wished would be present. It might possibly be for his good, and Banks had no particular desire to spare him. He turned a little out of his way to go up to Briton's Mead.

Banks found his sister hanging out clothes in the drying-ground behind the house.

"Well, Jack!" she said, as she caught sight of him.

"Is thy master within, Mall? If so be, I would have a word with him an' I may."

"Ay, he mostly is, these days. He's took to be terrible glum and grumpy. I'll go see if he'll speak with you."

"Tell him I bring news that it concerns him to hear."

Mary stopped and looked at him.

"Go thy ways, Mall. I said not, news it concerned thee to hear."

"Ay, but it doth! Jack, it is touching Mistress?"

"It is not ill news for her," replied Banks quietly.

"Then I know what you mean," said Mary, with a sob. "Oh, Jack, Jack! that we should have lived to see this day!"

She threw her apron over her face, and disappeared into the house. Banks waited a few minutes, till Mary returned with a disgusted face.

"You may go in, Jack; but 'tis a stone you'll find there."

Banks made his way to the dining-room, where Mr Benden was seated with a dish of cherries before him.

"'Day!" was all the greeting he vouchsafed.

"Good-day, Master. I am but now returned from Canterbury, where I have been in the Bishop's Court."

"Humph!" was the only expression of Mr Benden's interest. He had grown harder, colder, and stonier, since those days when he missed Alice's presence. He did not miss her now.

"The prisoners from this place were sentenced to-day."

"Humph!"

"They shall die there, the nineteenth of June next." Banks did not feel it at all necessary to soften his words, as he seemed to be addressing a stone wall.

"Humph!" The third growl sounded gruffer than the rest.

"And Mistress Benden said to Nichol Pardue—'Then shall we keep our Trinity octave in Heaven!'"

Mr Benden rose from his chair. Was he moved at last? What was he about to say? Thrusting forth a finger towards the door, he compressed his thanks and lamentations into a word—

"Go!"

John Banks turned away. Why should he stay longer?

"Poor soul!" was what he said, when he found himself again in the kitchen with Mary.

"What, *him*?" answered Mary rather scornfully.

"No—her, that she had to dwell with him. She'll have fairer company after Saturday."

"Is it Saturday, Jack?"

"Ay, Mall. Would you be there? I shall."

"No," said Mary, in a low tone. "I couldn't keep back my tears, and maybe they'd hurt her. She'll lack all her brave heart, and I'll not trouble her in that hour."

"You'd best not let Master Hall know—neither Mr Roger, nor Mr Thomas. It'd nigh kill poor little Mistress Christie to know of it aforehand. She loved her Aunt Alice so dearly."

"I can hold my tongue, Jack. Easier, maybe, than I can keep my hands off that wretch in yonder!"

When Mary went in to lay the cloth for the last meal, she found the wretch in question still seated at the table, his head buried in his hands. A gruffer voice than ever bade her "Let be! Keep away!" Mary withdrew quietly, and found it a shade easier to keep her hands off Mr Benden after that incident.

Chapter Thirty Two.

One summer day.

The nineteenth of June was the loveliest of summer days, even in the Martyrs' Field at Canterbury, in the hollow at the end of which the seven stakes were set up. The field is nearly covered now by the station of the London, Chatham, and Dover Railway, but the hollow can still be traced whence the souls of His faithful witnesses went up to God.

John Banks was early on the ground, and so secured a front place. The crowd grew apace, until half the field was covered. Not only residents of the city, but casual sight-seers, made up the bulk of it, the rather since it was somewhat dangerous to be absent, especially for a suspected person. From the neighbouring villages, too, many came in—the village squire and his dame in rustling silks, the parish priest in his cassock, the labourers and their wives in holiday garb.

Then the Castle gates opened, and the Wincheap Gate; and forth from them came a slow, solemn procession, preceded by a crucifer bearing a silver cross, a long array of black-robed priests, and then the Lord Bishop of Dover, in his episcopal robes, followed by two scarlet-cassocked acolytes swinging thuribles, from which ascended a cloud of incense between his Lordship's sacred person and the wicked heretics who were to follow. Two and two they came, John Fishcock the butcher, led like one of his own sheep to the slaughter, and Nicholas White the ironmonger; Nicholas Pardue and Sens Bradbridge; Mrs Final and Emmet Wilson. After all the rest came Alice Benden, on the last painful journey that she should ever take. She would mount next upon wings as an eagle, and there should for her be no more pain.

The martyrs recognised their friend John Banks, and each greeted him by a smile. Then they took off their outer garments—which were the perquisites of the executioners—and stood arrayed every one in that white robe of martyrdom, of which so many were worn in

Mary's reign; a long plain garment, falling from the throat to the feet, with long loose sleeves buttoned at the wrists. Thus prepared, they knelt down to pray, while the executioners heaped the faggots in the manner best suited for quick burning. Rising from their prayers, each was chained to a stake. Now was the moment for the last farewells.

John Banks went up to Alice Benden.

"Courage, my mistress, for a little time! and the Lord be with you!"

"Amen!" she answered. "I thank thee, Jack. Do any of my kin know of my burning?"

"Mistress, I told not your brethren, and methinks they wot not of the day. Methought it should be sore to them, and could do you but a little good. I pray you, take me as 'presenting all your friends, that do bid you right heartily farewell, and desire for you an abundant entrance into the happy kingdom of our Lord God."

"I thank thee with all mine heart, Jack; thou hast well done. Give, I pray thee, to my brother Roger this new shilling, the which my father sent me at my first imprisonment, desiring him that he will give the same unto mine old good father, in token that I never lacked money, with mine obedient salutations."

The gaoler now approached her to place the faggots closer, and Banks was reluctantly compelled to retire. From her waist Alice took a white lace which she had tied round it, and handed it to the gaoler, saying, "Keep this, I beseech you, for my brother Roger Hall. It is the last bond I was bound with, except this chain."

Then the torch was put to the faggots.

"Keep this in memory of me!" reached John Banks, in the clear tones of Alice Benden; and a white cambric handkerchief fluttered above the crowd, and fell into his outstretched hands. (These farewells of Alice Benden are historical.)

And so He led them to the haven where they would be.

> "No, not one looked back, who had set his hand to this ploughing!"

There was a hard task yet before John Banks. He had to visit eight houses, and at each to tell his awful tale, to father and mother, brother and sister, son and daughter—in three instances to husband or wife—of the martyrs who had gone home. His first visit was to Seven Roods.

"Well, Jack Banks! I thought you'd been dead and buried!" was Tabitha's sarcastic intimation that it was some time since she had seen him.

"Ah, Mistress Hall, I could well-nigh wish I had been, before I came to bring you such tidings as I bring to-day."

Tabitha looked up in his face, instantly dropped the mop in her hand, and came over to where he stood.

"'Tis more than 'may be,'" she said significantly, "and I reckon 'tis more than 'must be.' John Banks, is it *done*?"

"It is done," he replied. "'The Lord God hath wiped away all tears from her eyes.'"

"The Lord look upon it, and avenge her!" was the answer, in Tabitha's sternest and most solemn voice. "The Lord requite it on the head of Edward Benden, and on the head of Richard Thornton! Wherefore doth He not rend the heavens and come down? Wherefore—" and as suddenly as before, Tabitha broke down, and cried her heart out as Banks had never imagined Tabitha Hall could do.

Banks did not attempt to reprove her. It was useless. He only said quietly, "Forgive me to leave you thus, but I must be on my way, for my tidings must yet be told six times, and there be some hearts will break to hear them."

"I'll spare you one," said Tabitha, as well as she could speak. "You may let be Roger Hall. I'll tell him."

Banks drew a long breath. Could he trust this strange, satirical, yet warm-hearted woman to tell those tidings in that house of all others? And the white lace, which the gaoler, knowing him to be a Staplehurst man, had entrusted to him to give, could he leave it with her?

"Nay, not so, I pray you, and thank you, Mistress. I have an especial message and token for Master Hall. But if you would of your goodness let Mistress Final's childre know thereof, that should do me an easement, for the White Hart is most out of my way."

"So be it, Jack, and God speed thee!"

Turning away from Seven Roods, Banks did his terrible errand to the six houses. It was easiest at Fishcock's, where the relatives were somewhat more distant than at the rest; but hard to tell Nicholas White's grey-haired wife that she was a widow, hard to tell Emmet Wilson's husband that he had no more a wife; specially hard at Collet Pardue's cottage, where the news meant not only sorrow but worldly ruin, so far as mortal eye might see. Then he turned off to Briton's Mead, and told Mary, whose tears flowed fast.

"Will you speak to *him*?" she said, in an awed tone.

"No!" said Banks, almost sternly. "At the least—what doth he?"

"Scarce eats a morsel, and his bed's all awry in the morning, as if he'd done nought but toss about all the night; I think he sleeps none, or very nigh. I never speak to him without he first doth, and that's mighty seldom."

Banks hesitated a moment. Then he went forward, and opened the door of the dining-room.

"Mr Benden!" he said.

The room was in semi-darkness, having no light but that of the moon, and Banks could see only just enough to assure him that something human sat in the large chair at the further end. But no sound answered his appeal.

"I am but now arrived from Canterbury."

Still no answer came. John Banks went on, in a soft, hushed voice—not in his own words. If the heart of stone could be touched, God's words might do it; if not, still they were the best.

"'She shall hunger no more, neither thirst any more; neither shall the sun light upon her, neither any heat. For the Lamb that is in the midst of the Seat hath fed her, and hath led her unto fountains of living water; and God hath wiped away all tears from her eyes.'"

He paused a moment, but the dead silence was unbroken.

One word more. "The Lord have mercy on thy soul, thou miserable sinner!" Then Banks shut the door softly and went away.

There we leave Edward Benden, with the black silence of oblivion over his future life. Whether the Holy Spirit of God ever took the stony heart out of him, and gave him a heart of flesh, God alone knows. For this, in its main features, is a true story, and there is no word to tell us what became of the husband and betrayer of Alice Benden.

John Banks went on to the last house he had to visit—the little house by the Second Acre Close. Roger Hall opened the door himself. Banks stepped in, and as the light of the hall lantern fell upon his face, Roger uttered an exclamation of pain and fear.

"Jack! Thy face—"

"Hath my face spoken to you, Master Hall, afore my tongue could frame so to do? Perchance it is best so. Hold your hand."

Roger obeyed mechanically, and Banks laid on the hand held forth the long white lace.

"For you," he said, his voice broken by emotion. John Banks' nerves were pretty well worn out by that day's work, as well they might be. "She gave it me for you—at the last. She bade me say it was the last bond she was bound with—except *that* chain."

"Thank God!" were the first words that broke from the brother who loved Alice so dearly. The Christian spoke them; but the next moment the man came uppermost, and an exceeding bitter cry of "O Alice, Alice!" followed the thanksgiving of faith.

"It is over," said Banks, in a husky voice. "She 'shall never see evil any more.'"

But he knew well that he could give no comfort to that stricken heart. Quietly, and quickly, he laid down the new shilling, with its message for the poor old father; and then without another word—not even saying "good-night," he went out and closed the door behind him. Only God could speak comfort to Roger and Christabel in that dark hour. Only God could help poor Roger to tell Christie that she would never see her dear Aunt Alice any more until she should clasp hands with her on the street of the Golden City, and under the shade of the Tree of Life. And God would help him: John Banks was quite sure of that. But as he stepped out into the summer night, it seemed almost as if he could see a vision—as if the outward circumstances in which he had beheld the trio were prophetic—Alice in the glory of the great light, Roger with his way shown clearly by the little lamp of God's Word, and Edward in that black shadow, made lurid and more awful by the faint unearthly light. The moon came out brightly from behind a cloud, just as Banks lifted his eyes upwards.

"Good God, forgive us all!" he said earnestly, "and help all that need Thee!"

Alice was above all help, and Roger was sure of help. But who or what could help Edward Benden save the sovereign mercy of God?

Chapter Thirty Three.

What they could.

A month had passed since the burning of the Canterbury martyrs. The Bishop of Dover had gone on a visit to London, and the land had rest in his absence. It may be noted here, since we shall see no more of him, that he did not long survive the event. He was stricken suddenly with palsy, as he stood watching a game at bowls on a Sunday afternoon, and was borne to his bed to die. The occupation wherein the "inevitable angel" found him, clearly shows what manner of man he was.

In Roger Hall's parlour a little conclave was gathered for discussion of various subjects, consisting of the handful of Gospellers yet left in Staplehurst. Various questions had been considered, and dismissed as settled, and the conversation flagged for a few seconds, when Tabitha suddenly flung a new topic into the arena.

"Now, what's to be done for that shiftless creature, Collet Pardue? Six lads and two lasses, and two babes of Sens Bradbridge's, and fewer wits than lads, and not so many pence as lasses. Won't serve to find 'em all dead in the gutter. So what's to be done? Speak up, will you, and let's hear."

"I can't speak on those lines, Tabitha," replied her brother-in-law. "Collet is no wise shiftless, for she hath brought up her children in a good and godly fashion, the which a woman with fewer brains than lads should ne'er have done. But I verily assent with you that we should do something to help her. And first—who will take to Sens Bradbridge's maids?"

"I will, if none else wants 'em. But they'll not be pampered and stuffed with cates, and lie on down beds, and do nought, if they dwell with me. I shall learn 'em to fare hard and be useful, I can tell you."

"Whether of the twain call you them syllabubs and custard pies as you set afore us when we supped last with you, Mistress Hall?" quietly asked Ursula Final. "Seemed to me I could put up with hard fare o' that sort metely well."

"Don't be a goose, Ursula. They've got to keep their hands in, a-cooking, haven't they? and when things be made, you can't waste 'em nor give 'em the pigs. They've got to be ate, haven't they?" demanded Mrs Tabitha, in tones of battle; and Ursula subsided without attempting a defence.

"What say you, Tom?" asked Roger, looking at his brother.

Mr Thomas Hall, apparently, did not dare to say anything. He glanced deprecatingly at his domestic tyrant, and murmured a few words, half swallowed in the utterance, of which "all agree" were the only distinguishable syllables.

"Oh, he'll say as I say," responded Tabitha unblushingly. "There's no man in the Weald knows his duty better than Thomas Hall; it'd be a mercy if he'd sometimes do it."

Mr Thomas Hall's look of meek appeal said "Don't I?" in a manner which was quite pathetic.

"Seems to me," said Ralph Final, the young landlord of the White Hart, "that if we were all to put of a hat or a bowl such moneys as we could one and another of us afford by the year, for Mistress Pardue and the childre—such as could give money, look you—and them that couldn't should say what they would give, it'd be as plain a way as any."

"Well said, Ralph!" pronounced Mrs Tabitha, who took the lead as usual. "I'll give my maids' cast-off clothes for the childre, the elder, I mean, such as 'll fit 'em; the younger must go for Patience and Charity. And I'll let 'em have a quart of skim milk by the day, as oft as I have it to spare; and eggs if I have 'em. And Thomas 'll give 'em ten shillings by the year. And I shouldn't marvel if I can make up a kirtle or a hood for Collet by nows and thens, out of some gear of my own."

Mr Thomas Hall being looked at by the Synod to see if he assented, confirmed the statement of his arbitrary Tabitha by a submissive nod.

"I'll give two nobles by the year," said Ralph, "and a peck of barley by the quarter, and a cask of beer at Christmas."

"I will give them a sovereign by the year," said Roger Hall, "and half a bale of cloth from the works, that Master suffers me to buy at cost price."

"I can't do so much as you," said Eleanor White, the ironmonger's widow; "but I'll give Collet the worth of an angel in goods by the year, and the produce of one of the pear-trees in my garden."

"I can't do much neither," added Emmet Wilson's husband, the baker; "but I'll give them a penn'orth of bread by the week, and a peck of meal at Easter."

"And I'll chop all the wood they burn," said his quiet, studious son Titus, "and learn the lads to read."

"Why, Titus, you are offering the most of us all in time and labour!" exclaimed Roger Hall.

"You've got your work cut and measured, Titus Wilson," snapped Tabitha. "If one of them lads'll bide quiet while you can drum ABC into his head that it'll tarry there a week, 'tis more than I dare look for, I can tell you."

"There's no telling what you can do without you try," was the pithy answer of Titus.

"I've been marvelling what I could do," said John Banks modestly, "and I was a bit beat out of heart by your sovereigns and nobles; for I couldn't scarce make up a crown by the year. But Titus has showed me the way. I'll learn one of the lads my trade, if Collet 'll agree."

"Well, then, that is all we can do, it seems—" began Roger, but he was stopped by a plaintive voice from the couch.

"Mightn't I do something, Father? I haven't only a sixpence in money; but couldn't I learn Beatrice to embroider, if her mother would spare her?"

"My dear heart, it were to try thy strength too much, I fear," said Roger tenderly.

"But you're all doing something," said Christie earnestly, "and wasn't our blessed Lord weary when He sat on the well? I might give Him a little weariness, mightn't I—when I've got nothing better?"

To the surprise of everybody, Thomas had replied.

"We're not doing much, measured by that ell-wand," said the silent man; "but Titus and Banks and Christie, they're doing the most."

Poor Collet Pardue broke down in a confused mixture of thanks and tears, when she heard the propositions of her friends. She was gratefully willing to accept all the offers. Three of her boys were already employed at the cloth-works; one of the younger trio should go to Banks to be brought up a mason. Which would he choose?

Banks looked at the three lads offered him—the noisy Noah, the ungovernable Silas, and the lazy Valentine.

"I'll have Silas," he said quietly.

"The worst pickle of the lot!" commented Mrs Tabitha, who made one of the deputation.

"Maybe," said Banks calmly; "but I see wits there, and I'll hope for a heart, and with them and the grace of God, which Collet and I shall pray for, we'll make a man of Silas Pardue yet."

And if John Banks ever regretted his decision, it was not on a certain winter evening, well into the reign of Elizabeth, when a fine, manly-looking fellow, with a grand forehead wherein "his soul lodged well," and bright intellectual eyes, came to tell him, the humble mason, that he had been chosen from a dozen candidates for the high post of architect of a new church.

"'Tis your doing," said the architect, as he wrung the hard hand of the mason. "You made a man of me by your teaching and praying, and never despairing that I should one day be worth the cost."

But we must return for a few minutes to Roger Hall's parlour, where he and his little invalid girl were alone on that night when the conference had been held.

"Father," said Christie, "please tell me what is a cross? and say it little, so as I can conceive the same."

"What manner of cross, sweet heart?"

"You know what our Lord saith, Father—'He that taketh not his cross, and followeth Me, is not worthy of Me.' I've been thinking a deal on it of late. I wouldn't like not to be worthy of Him. But I can't take my cross till I know what it is. I asked Cousin Friswith, and she said it meant doing all manner of hard disagreeable things, like the monks and nuns do—eating dry bread and sleeping of a board, and such like. But when I talked with Pen Pardue, she said she reckoned it signified not that at all. That was making crosses, and our Lord did not mention that. So please, Father, what is it?"

"Methinks, my child, Pen hath the right. 'Take' is not 'make.' We be to take the cross God layeth on our backs. He makes the crosses; we have but to take them and bear them. Folks make terrible messes by times when they essay to make their own crosses. But thou wouldest know what is a cross? Well, for thee, methinks, anything that cometh across thee and makes thee cross. None wist so well as thyself what so doth."

"But, Father!" said Christie in a tone of alarm.

"Well, sweet heart?"

"There must be such a lot of them!"

"For some folks, Christie, methinks the Lord carveth out one great heavy cross; but for others He hath, as it were, an handful of little light ones, that do but weigh a little, and prick a little, each one. And he knoweth which to give."

"I think," said Christie, with an air of profound meditation, "I must have the little handful. But then, must I carry them all at once?"

"One at once, little Christie—the one which thy Father giveth thee; let Him choose which, and how, and when. By times he may give thee more than one, but methinks mostly 'tis one at once, though they may change oft and swiftly. Take *thy* cross, and follow the Lord Jesus."

"There's banging doors," pursued Christie with the same thoughtful air; "that's one. And when my back aches, that's another, and when my head is so, *so* tired; and when I feel all strings that somebody's pulling, as if I couldn't keep still a minute. That last's one of the biggest, I reckon. And when—"

The little voice stopped suddenly for a moment.

"Father, can folks be crosses?"

"I fear they can, dear heart," replied her father, smiling; "and very sharp ones too."

Christie kept her next thoughts to herself. Aunt Tabitha and Cousin Friswith certainly must be crosses, she mentally decided, and Uncle Edward must have been dear Aunt Alice's cross, and a dreadful one. Then she came back to the point in hand.

"How must I 'take up' my cross, Father? Doth it mean I must not grumble at it, and feel as if I wanted to get rid of it as fast as ever I could?"

Roger smiled and sighed. "That is hard work, Christie, is it not? But it would be no cross if it were not hard and heavy. Thou canst not but feel that it will be a glad thing to lay it down; but now, while God layeth it on thee, be willing to bear it for His sake. He giveth it for thy sake, that thou mayest be made partaker of His holiness; be thou ready to carry it for His. 'The cup which My Father hath given Me, shall I not drink it?'"

"There'll be no crosses and cups in heaven, will there, Father?"

"Not one, Christabel."

"Only crowns and harps?" the child went on thoughtfully. "Aunt Alice has both, Father. I think she must make right sweet music. I hope I sha'n't be far from her. Perhaps it won't be very long before I hear her. Think you it will, Father?"

Little Christabel had no idea what a sharp cross she had laid on her father's heart by asking him that question. Roger Hall had to fight with himself before he answered it, and it was scarcely to her that his reply was addressed.

"'Not as I will, but as Thou wilt.' 'He knoweth the way that I take.' 'I will not fail thee, neither forsake thee.'"

"Oh, Father, what pretty verses! Were you thinking perhaps you'd miss me if I went soon, poor Father? But maybe, I sha'n't, look you. 'Tis only when I ache so, and feel all over strings, sometimes I think— But we don't know, Father, do we? And we shall both be there, you know. It won't signify much, will it, which of us goes first?"

"It will only signify," said Roger huskily, "to the one that tarrieth."

"Well," answered Christie brightly, "and it won't do that long. I reckon we scarce need mind."

Chapter Thirty Four.

Once more at home.

Up and down his garden—or, to speak more accurately, his brother's garden—strolled Mr Justice Roberts, his hands behind his back, on a mild afternoon at the beginning of December 1558. His thoughts, which of course we have the privilege of reading, ran somewhat in this fashion—

"Well, 'tis a mercy all is pretty well settled now. Nothing but joy and welcome for the Queen's accession. Every man about, pretty nigh, looks as if he had been released from prison, and was so thankful he scarce knew how to express it. To be sure there be a few contradictious folks that would fain have had the old fashions tarry; but, well-a-day! they be but an handful. I'll not say I'm not glad myself. I never did love committing those poor wretches that couldn't believe to order. *I* believe in doing your duty and letting peaceable folks be. If they do reckon a piece of bread to be a piece of bread, I'd never burn them for it."

By this reflection it will be seen that Mr Justice Roberts, in his heart, was neither a Papist nor a Protestant, but a good-natured Gallio, whose convictions were pliable when wanted so to be.

"I marvel how soon I shall hear of Tom," the Justice's meditations went on. "I cannot let him know anything, for I don't know where he is; I rather guess at Shardeford, with his wife's folks, but I had a care not to find out. He'll hear, fast enough, that it is safe to come home. I shouldn't wonder—"

The Justice wheeled round suddenly, and spoke aloud this time. "Saints alive! what's that?"

Nothing either audible or visible appeared for a moment.

"What was that black thing?" said the Justice to himself. He was answered suddenly in loud tones of great gratification.

"Bow-wow! Bow-wow-wow! Bow-ow-ow-ow-ow!"

"Whatever!" said the Justice to the "black thing" which was careering about him, apparently on every side of him at once, leaping into the air as high as his head, trying to lick his face, wagging not only a feathery tail, but a whole body, laughing all over a delighted face, and generally behaving itself in a rapturously ecstatic manner. "Art thou rejoicing for Queen Elizabeth too? and whose dog art thou? Didst come—tarry, I do think—nay—ay, it is—I verily believe 'tis old Jack himself!"

"Of course it is!" said Jack's eyes and tail, and every bit of Jack, executing a fresh caper of intense satisfaction.

"Why, then they must be come!" exclaimed the Justice, and set off for the front door, pursued by Jack. It is needless to say that Jack won the race by considerable lengths.

"Oh, here's Uncle Anthony!" cried Pandora's voice, as he came in sight. "Jack, you've been and told him—good Jack!"

There is no need to describe the confused, heart-warm greetings on all sides—how kisses were exchanged, and hands were clasped, and sentences were begun that were never finished, and Jack assisted at all in turn. But when the first welcomes were over, and the travellers had changed their dress, and they sat down to supper, hastily got up by Margery's willing hands, there was opportunity to exchange real information on both sides.

"And where have you been, now, all this while?" asked the Justice. "I never knew, and rather wished not to guess."

"At Shardeford, for the first part; then some months with Frances, and lately in a farm-house under Ingleborough—folks that Frances knew, good Gospellers, but far from any priest. And how have matters gone here?"

"There's nought, methinks, you'll be sorry to hear of, save only the burnings at Canterbury. Seven from this part—Mistress Benden, and Mistress Final, Fishcock, White, Pardue, Emmet Wilson, and Sens Bradbridge. They all suffered a few weeks after your departing."

All held their breath till the list was over. Pandora was the first to speak.

"Oh, my poor little Christie!"

"Your poor little Christie, Mistress Dorrie, is like to be less poor than she was. There is a doctor of medicine come to dwell in Cranbrook, that seems to have somewhat more skill, in her case at least, than our old apothecary; and you shall find the child going about the house now. He doth not despair, quoth he, that she may yet walk forth after a quiet fashion, though she is not like to be a strong woman at the best."

"Oh, I am so glad, Uncle!" said Pandora, though the tears *were* still in her eyes.

"That Roger Hall is a grand fellow, Tom. He hath kept the works a-going as if you had been there every day. He saith not much, but he can do with the best."

"Ay, he was ever a trustworthy servant," answered Mr Roberts. "'Tis a marvel to me, though, that he was never arrest."

"That cannot I conceive!" said the Justice warmly. "The man hath put his head into more lions' mouths than should have stocked Daniel's den; and I know Dick o' Dover set forth warrants for his taking. It did seem as though he bare a charmed life, that no man could touch him."

"He is not the first that hath so done," said Mistress Grena. "Methinks, Master Justice, there was another warrant sent out first—'I am with thee, and no man shall set on thee to hurt thee.' There have been divers such, I count, during Queen Mary's reign."

"Maybe, Mistress Grena, maybe; I am not o'er good in such matters. But I do think, Brother Tom, you should do well to show your sense of Hall's diligence and probity."

"That will I do, if God permit. But there is another to whom I owe thanks, Anthony, and that is yourself, to have saved my lands and goods for me."

"Well, Tom," answered the Justice comically, "you do verily owe me thanks, to have eaten your game, and worn out your furniture, and spent your money, during an whole year and an half. Forsooth, I scarce know how you may fitly show your gratefulness toward me for conferring so great benefits upon you."

Mr Roberts laughed.

"Ah, it pleaseth you to jest, Anthony," he replied, "but I know full well that had you refused my request, 'tis a mighty likelihood I had had neither house nor furniture to come to."

"Nay, I was not such a dolt! I marvel who would, when asked to spend another man's money, and pluck his fruit, and lie of his best bed! But I tell thee one thing, Tom—I'll pay thee never a stiver of rent for mine house that I hold of thee—the rather since I let it to this new doctor for two pound more, by the year, than I have paid to thee. I'm none so sure that he'll be ready to turn forth; and if no, happy man be my dole, for I must go and sing in the gutter, without Jack will give me a corner of his kennel."

"Jack's owner will be heartily glad to give you a corner of his kennel, Brother Anthony, for so long time as it shall please you to occupy it. Never think on turning forth, I pray you, until you desire to go, at the least while I live."

"I thank you right truly, Brother Tom, and will take my advantage of your kindliness at least for this present. But, my young mistresses, I pray you remember that you must needs be of good conditions an' you dwell in the same house with a Justice of Peace, else shall I be forced to commit you unto gaol."

"Oh, we'll keep on the windy side of you and the law, Uncle Anthony," said Gertrude, laughing. "I suppose teasing the life out of one's uncle is not a criminal offence?"

"I shall do my best to make it so, my lady," was the reply, in tones of mock severity.

The rest of the day was devoted to unpacking and settling down, and much of the next morning was spent in a similar manner. But when the afternoon came Pandora rode down, escorted by old Osmund, to Roger Hall's cottage. She was too familiar there now for the ceremony of waiting to ring; and she went forward and opened the door of the little parlour.

Christabel was standing at the table arranging some floss silk—"slea-silk" she would have called it—in graduated shades for working. It was the first time Pandora had ever seen her stand. Down went the delicate pale green skein in Christie's hand, and where it might go was evidently of no moment.

"Mistress Pandora! O dear Mistress Pandora! You've come back! I hadn't heard a word about it. And look you, I can stand! and I can walk!" cried Christie, in tones of happy excitement.

"My dear little Christabel!" said Pandora, clasping the child in her arms. "I am surely glad for thy betterment—very, very glad. Ay, sweet heart, we have come home, all of us, thank God!"

"And you'll never go away again, will you, Mistress Pandora?"

"'Never' is a big word, Christie. But I hope we shall not go again for a great while."

"Oh, and did anybody tell you, Mistress—about—poor Aunt Alice?" said Christie, with a sudden and total change of tone.

"No, Christie," answered Pandora significantly. "But somebody told me touching thy rich Aunt Alice, that she was richer now and higher than even the Queen Elizabeth, and that she should never again lose her riches, nor come down from her throne any more."

"We didn't know, Mistress—Father and me, we never knew when it should be—we only heard when all was over!"

"Thou mightest well bless God for that, my dear heart. That hour would have been sore hard for thee to live through, hadst thou known it afore."

The parlour door opened, and they saw Roger Hall standing in the doorway.

"Mistress Pandora!" he said. "Thanks be unto God for all His mercies!"

"Amen!" answered both the girls.

"Methinks, Mr Hall, under God, some thanks be due to you also," remarked Pandora, with a smile. "Mine aunt and I had fared ill without your pots and pans that time you wot of, and mine uncle hath been ringing your praises in my Father's ears touching your good management at the cloth-works."

"I did but my duty, Mistress," said Roger, modestly.

"I would we all did the same, Mr Hall, so well as you have done," added Pandora. "Christie, my sister Gertrude saith she will come and see thee."

"Oh!" answered Christie, with an intonation of pleasure. "Please, Mistress Pandora, is she as good as you?"

Both Roger and Pandora laughed.

"How must I answer, Christie?" said the latter. "For, if I say 'ay,' that shall be to own myself to be good; and if 'no,' then were it to speak evil of my sister. She is brighter and cheerier than I, and loveth laughter and mirth. Most folks judge her to be the fairer and sweeter of the twain."

"I shall not," said Christie, with a shake of her head; "of that am I very certain."

Roger privately thought he should not either.

"Well," said Christie, "I do hope any way, *now*, all our troubles be over! Please, Mistress Pandora, think you not they shall be?"

"My dear little maid!" answered Pandora, laughing.

"Not without we be in Heaven, Christie," replied her Father, "and methinks we have scarce won thither yet."

Christabel looked extremely disappointed.

"Oh, dear!" she said, "I made sure we should have no more, now Queen Elizabeth was come in. Must we wait, then, till we get to Heaven, Father?"

"Wait till we reach Heaven, sweet heart, for the land where we shall no more say, 'I am sick,' either in health or heart. It were not good for us to walk ever in the plains of ease; we should be yet more apt than we be to build our nests here, and forget to stretch our wings upward toward Him who is the first cause and the last end of all hope and goodness. 'Tis only when we wake up after His likeness, to be with Him for ever, that we shall be satisfied with it."

The End.

Lightning Source UK Ltd.
Milton Keynes UK
07 November 2009

145947UK00001B/98/P